Sand Dollars

EVELYN GRACE

Lana -
Thank you for
your support! My
God continue to help you
through the storms of life.

Lisa B

(aka Evelyn Grace)

Jeremiah 29:11

Sand Dollars

Trade paperback ISBN 978-1-7345735-4-1
eBook AISN B096PPXQTV

All scripture quotations are taken from the New
American Standard Bible® (NASB) Copyright © 1960,
1962, 1963, 1968, 1971, 1972, 1973, 1975, 1977, 1995 by
the Lockman Foundation. Used by permission.
www.Lockman.org

Cover design: K&J Couture Designs
https://www.behance.net/kjcdesignsme

Author photo: ©Click and Capture Photography

For my wonderful husband
Bobby

Thank you for always being my safe place
in every storm — my haven.

Table of Contents

Peace I leave you,
My peace I give you; not as the world gives,
do I give to you.
Do not let your hearts be troubled,
nor fearful.
John 14:27

There is no fear in love;
but perfect love casts out fear
1 John 4:18

ONE

He slammed his fist on the steering wheel. He had miscalculated and he made it a point never to do that. He had told her. He had warned her. She knew the risks of defying him.

He hadn't thought she would be able to slip out of his grasp so easily. He had worked hard to ensure she would understand there was no going back once she was his.

He had been embarrassed to show up at work this morning to find out she was gone. He did not like surprises.

His eyes burned as he now stared at the dark windows of her apartment. He'd come just to confirm what he already knew. She had left, but he'd find her. She couldn't hide from him. She just didn't know it yet.

Bryce set his mouth in a grim line as he turned the key to start his car. She would regret the day she decided to leave him. He would make sure of it.

*****

Sabrina Martin began muttering under her breath. The car had done fine all the way north on I-95. For the last few miles though, something was off. She watched as the temperature gauge slowly climbed. She wished now she'd thought to get it checked before she left, but there hadn't been time.

She shook her head. She had promised herself she was going to stop second guessing every decision. How was she supposed to have known something would go wrong on the long drive? Her confidence had taken a beating over the last year.

She just needed to get to the next town. Hopefully, there would be a garage there. Then the car could die. Better yet maybe the issue would just go away on its own.

She had been driving all night and had spent most of that time having second thoughts. Should she turn back? No, she had to go forward. She was scared to return and just as scared to keep going.

Fear had ruled her life for far too long. It was time to make changes. Every time she convinced herself of this, she would once more begin to shrink at the thought of all that could go wrong.

It wasn't until she crossed the bridge to Maine that she'd felt the tightness in her chest ease. It wasn't until the sight of the long, green metal bridge with its "Welcome to Maine: The Way Life Should Be" sign when she felt a small bit of peace come over her.

Returning to the state where she had grown up finally felt right. She wouldn't let the fear she was facing stop her. Not this time.

Sabrina was done stuffing fear and anxiety down. She had finally seen the truth. She shook her head and pushed the thoughts to the back of her mind. She wouldn't dwell on it. If she

3

did, she was afraid she'd pull over and never move again.

She was hopeful her departure had gone unnoticed, for a little while at least. She wasn't sure what she would do if it hadn't. If he came after her…the thought trailed off. No, she wasn't going to go there. Not now.

Sabrina watched as the temperature gauge continue to climb. She knew something was wrong. She began talking out loud to calm herself. "Come on. I just need to make it to the next town. Please, let me get there."

She gripped the steering wheel tightly between her hands as if to add her own will to the car as she continued to repeat her pleas. She wasn't sure if she was asking God or just the universe in general. She didn't know anymore.

She'd once believed, but it seemed like ages ago now. She couldn't pinpoint the moment when she stopped talking with God. It was such a gradual change. She'd once trusted Him completely with her life, but now? Now she didn't even trust herself to decide something as minor as what color lipstick to wear.

She shook off the thoughts once more and focused on putting some positive energy into the car. She kept urging it on, hoping it wouldn't die until she was somewhere safe.

Sabrina knew she must be getting closer to one of the small towns that meandered their way up the coast. She hoped there was some type of garage with someone who could help her figure out what was wrong and get her back on the road.

She decided on the long drive that she wasn't going back to her hometown. There was no family left there anyway. All her relatives now either lived out of state after the paper mill closed or had since died. The old town hadn't had much going for it when she was a child. It had even less now.

As an adult she would be hard pressed to find meaningful employment. Better to start fresh elsewhere.

She needed to work on finding her confidence. She wasn't even sure what changed to make her so insecure and scared. She stopped herself.

That wasn't true. Sabrina knew she needed to face the lies she once believed to be truth. She needed to strip it all away and see what was really in front of her, what everyone else knew.

Had everyone at work been laughing behind her back at her? Had they known his true nature? Why hadn't anyone warned her? Would she have listened to them? The questions kept swirling through her mind.

He'd done such a good job of isolating her from anyone she might have called friend that there wasn't anyone she could trust. She needed to face the truth of it all. Everything changed the day she met *him*. Her thoughts continued spinning as she considered all that was different.

Just as Sabrina felt herself spiraling down the "what if" path again, she saw a sign proclaiming, "Welcome to Haven. A Small Piece of Heaven."

"Thank goodness!" She smiled broadly as she soon spotted the sign for a garage, the Ritz Gas 'N Go, a mile up the road. She was safe. Maybe. She just needed to drive a few more minutes.

"Come on, you can do it!" She patted the dashboard and smiled ruefully as she realized she was now reduced to talking to her car.

As she put on her blinker to turn, steam began billowing from under the hood. Just in the nick of time. She'd been so afraid she would get stranded somewhere between Connecticut and Maine that she hardly even stopped to rest.

She stepped out of the car and saw an older man striding across the parking lot. She wondered if God had been listening after all.

"Looks like you might be in need of some help." The man grinned as he reached her and stuck out a hand. "Name's Darren Ritz. What seems to be the problem?"

Sabrina shook his hand. "I'm Sabrina, Sabrina Martin, but you can call me Bree."

She stepped back from the smoking car and shrugged her shoulders. "No idea. It was running fine until a few miles back. Now this." She pointed toward the hood as steam continued to billow out.

"Let's pop the hood and take a look."

Sabrina reached in and fumbled for the hood release. The man gingerly reached around under the hood to find the lever and soon had it propped open.

Sabrina looked over as another man came hurrying across the lot towards them. "Be careful there, Darren. Don't need you getting burned so early in the day."

Both men soon had their heads under the hood as they poked and prodded, looking for the issue. Sabrina stood quietly to the side in the hot July sun. It was going to be a scorcher today if it already felt this warm so early in the morning.

"You're not going to be driving this again today. Want us to take a look and see what we can do to get it going again?"

Sabrina's head snapped up. She'd been deep in thought about how she would manage her expenses. She had some money saved, but she would need to find a job soon. And she hadn't planned on car repairs so early in her escape. Her intention was to go further north, find a place to live, a job, and figure out a way to live a normal life again.

"Yeah, I'd really appreciate that. Can you get me an estimate before you do anything?"

"Sure thing. You're not from around here, are you?" She saw the men checking out the bags and boxes in her backseat. She had tossed in what she could grab in a hurry. She hadn't had time to pack properly and it showed.

Yesterday, when her world shifted. Yesterday, when the veil of lies had fully been removed. Yesterday, when she realized she had to leave. Immediately. Yesterday…she shook her head slightly and brightened her smile.

9

"No, I'm from over by Bangor. I've been away for a while and I'm moving back. Know anywhere I could stay? Or anyone who might be hiring?"

"You can try the Three Cats Café. It's just down the way there. Easy enough walk. Our sisters own it. They just mentioned they were looking for another waitress. They might know of a place to rent, too. There isn't much that goes around here that they don't know about. If anyone can help you, they can."

Sabrina snagged her purse from the front seat and pulled her cell phone off the charging cord. "Thanks, I'll check back tomorrow about my car." The men nodded as they once more started poking around.

She smiled to herself as she started off at a brisk pace down the road to find the café. Now was as good as time as any for a fresh start. It was time for her to figure out who she was without a man in her life. She needed to find her strength and confidence again.

TWO

Lucas Grant sighed as he sat in his cruiser. He knew he'd moved to Haven for a slower pace, but this was getting ridiculous. The most exciting thing he'd dealt with so far this week was a little boy who had wandered too far from his mom at the local grocery store. As soon as he pulled in to join the search, the little guy popped around the corner and yelled, "Found you!"

He rested his head on the back of the seat and closed his eyes. Moving to Maine from Miami had seemed like a good idea. This was where his family used to spend summers when he was a kid. Both of his older brothers now lived here. It was nice to be around family again.

A quieter beat seemed just what he needed after, well, after everything. He opened his eyes and shook his head. He needed to stop dwelling on the past. It didn't change anything. It never would.

He sighed as he put the vehicle into drive and headed out to do another round. The tourist season was in full swing, making the population of Haven almost triple what it would be in the fall and winter. During the summer it seemed there were people everywhere. On the off season, they were sometimes harder to find.

"Okay, Lord. You told me this was where you wanted me, so here I am. Now what? I could use a little bit of excitement in my life. Not too much though. I'm counting on you to get the right amount."

His eyes scanned the people meandering down the sidewalks and lounging on the beach as he slowly cruised along the ocean front. He rolled down his front windows and inhaled deeply. That smell never got old. The sea had its own scent and today it was just what he needed.

He knew winter would be here before he was ready. It was one reason he'd moved north. Having grown up in Florida, he thought he'd love the change of seasons.

He did love spring and fall. He was completely wrong about winter though. He thought he would love snow, but it was cold and wet and got everywhere. And he did mean *everywhere.*

He spent most of November through February trying to put on enough layers to keep warm but not so many he felt like he was waddling around like a penguin. It seemed he never felt truly warm again until the end of April when the threat of snow was finally gone.

He didn't like to remember last winter when a surprise storm dropped a few inches at the start of May. May! He shook his head at the thought. He hadn't realized moving to Maine could feel like living at the North Pole at times.

He continued to make his way past the boardwalk until he could turn towards the center of town. He planned to stop at the

Three Cats Café to grab more coffee and something to eat. He had skipped breakfast this morning and his stomach was letting him know how unhappy it was about that fact.

He was glad he was only part-time on the force. Haven had a few extra officers in the summer, which allowed Lucas to continue with his part-time status. While he enjoyed being a police officer, he knew he didn't have it in him anymore to work the job full-time.

He enjoyed the days he worked with his brother. Drew owned a handyman business making minor repairs and doing small projects. Tomorrow they were working on Agnes Johnson's house.

Lucas gave a short laugh. That woman thought she was the queen of Haven. It was her way or the highway but somehow his brother could always sweet talk her.

Someday Lucas would have to get him to share his secrets since he certainly couldn't do anything right around that woman. Of course, not many could. He'd witnessed Mrs. Johnson dressing down many citizens of Haven in the short time he lived here.

Just this morning, Lucas told Drew he would no longer work on Mrs. Johnson's house without his brother there. Lucas had made that mistake only once.

Mrs. Johnson had spent almost the entire day telling him everything he was doing wrong. He'd bitten his tongue, but he wasn't going to suffer through that again.

Haven was his home now. He enjoyed it. Really. Okay, so he was talking himself into liking it, but he'd only been here about a year now. It took time to adjust.

After all, Miami and Haven were completely opposite. Haven didn't have a single skyscraper. No violent crime. No gangs. While there were some drug issues, it wasn't like it was in the big city. The last time the police force here had dealt with a murder was more than thirty years ago.

No, this was good. He needed time to heal and come to terms with how he had failed his

partner. Antonio would still be here if only…
Lucas allowed his thoughts to trail off.
Dwelling on what might have been wouldn't
bring his partner back. Nothing could change
the past.

He'd come to terms with everything or so
he thought. He wished Antonio were back in
his life, but Jillian? Would he really change
things there? No, he had finally seen her true
self and he didn't want any part of it.

He wasn't even sure he ever wanted to be in
another relationship. He was having a hard
time trusting another woman. He was horrible
at reading between the lines and hated playing
games. And that's what dating felt like, one big
game.

And yet, over the last few months, he felt
God moving in his heart. Lucas knew it was
time to be open to the possibility of a
relationship again. He had watched Drew as he
moved toward his wedding to Kate. Lucas
wanted that type of relationship. One full of
trust and love for each other. He was working

to give his dating life over to God. It wasn't easy.

He kept driving, once more talking quietly to God about needing help. He needed a change. Something. He wasn't sure what it was, but he knew he could trust God to do the right thing. Just like always.

Lucas had proven he couldn't do it on his own. He had taken charge of his life once, thinking he knew how to live it better than the God of the Universe. He'd proven how untrue that was.

He made one more turn around the boardwalk and then headed towards the café. His stomach gave a gurgle of appreciation at the thought of some pastries.

Lucas smiled. There were some great things about living in Haven. The Three Cats Café was one of them.

THREE

Despite the short walk from the garage, Sabrina was thankful for the wash of cold air over her skin as she pushed open the door of the Three Cat Café. She was glad to be out of the humid air. Maine was a great place to be in the summer, but there were days when the humidity made it downright unbearable. Today was one of those days.

She looked around, taking in the quaint café. The place gave off a fifties diner vibe. There was a long low counter taking up most of the space along one side with stools in front. The kitchen was tucked in the back at one end. Booths were lined up along the plate glass windows overlooking the ocean. More tables and booths went around the corner.

The café had a casual, beach theme. There were fishing nets draped artfully on the walls with framed photographs of the ocean, dunes, and boardwalk hanging on them. Each table and booth had a small collection of shells and sand dollars on the tables with short ceramic vases holding flowers.

Sabrina turned to look for a restroom. She was hoping for a chance to freshen up before meeting the owner.

"Just one?" Sabrina jumped as she heard a voice behind her. She hadn't seen anyone nearby when she'd entered.

"Yes, well, actually no." Sabrina smiled at the young hostess. "I was wondering if I could talk to someone about a job. I was told there might be an opening here." Sabrina smoothed down the front of her wrinkled shirt. It looked like it was too late to do anything about her rumpled appearance now.

"Oh, sure! Let me go get one of the owners." The hostess started to walk away, turning back before she left.

"Um, the bathroom is right over there if you'd like to go freshen up a little. You look, well, you look a little melted." She smiled with sympathy at Sabrina as she left.

"Thanks!" Sabrina called after the girl as she shrugged her purse strap a little higher. She hurried towards the restroom hoping she wasn't beyond repair at this point.

Sabrina was thankful it was a single room as she slid the bolt home. Turning to look at herself in the mirror over the sink, she gave herself a wry smile. Melted was an apt description. Between the humidity and her lack of sleep, her appearance did not recommend her as a job applicant.

Haven. What was she doing here? She'd planned to head further north, closer to where she'd grown up, where she knew the location better. She'd once lived surrounded by fields and pine trees, not coastal inlets and rocky coasts.

She didn't know what would happen next, but the name of the town seemed to be calling to her. Haven. Peace. Safety. That was what she needed. A safe place to rest. She felt battered and emotionally drained. She was tired of being afraid.

Sabrina rubbed her hands together under the cool water and leaned down to splash her face. Rummaging through her purse she came up with a stick of deodorant which she quickly swiped on. She found an old tube of lipstick with some color left and applied that as well.

Another pass through her bottomless purse found a brush and, thankfully, a random hair elastic. She quickly ran the brush through her hair and pulled it up in a high ponytail. She couldn't do much for her clothing. She hoped her casual attire wouldn't count against her.

She felt a bit more refreshed outwardly at least. Inwardly, she still felt rather rumpled, but there wasn't much she could do about that just yet.

"Let's do this." She smiled at her reflection, hoping for a much needed confidence boost. Taking a deep breath, she unlocked the door

21

and headed back towards the front where she could see an older woman waiting beside the young hostess.

"Hello, I'm Sabrina Martin, but you can call me Bree. It's nice to meet you." She reached out a hand towards the woman who clasped it firmly in return. She wanted to make up for her appearance with a professional manner.

"Welcome, I'm Abigail Johnson, one of the owners. Rosie tells me you're looking for a job. Shall we go sit?"

Abigail led Sabrina towards a booth in an empty back corner. The café was quiet. The breakfast rush was already finished up and it wasn't quite yet time for lunch.

"So, Bree Martin, what brings you to my café today?"

Bree took a deep breath. "I was heading north, more inland actually. I was planning to relocate up near Bangor where I grew up, but my car picked Haven. It died on the way into town. Your brothers sent me in your direction

22

when I mentioned I was looking for a job and a place to stay."

She watched as the older woman thought about this statement. Had it been the right answer? She hoped so.

"Do you have any waitressing experience?"

"Not really, but I'm a fast learner and good with people." Bree knew experience often mattered, but she only hoped Abigail wouldn't care. How hard could the job be anyway?

"We do have an opening for a part-time waitress. It's mostly mornings with some afternoons and weekends as needed. One of our girls met someone and moved to the Portland area. We're short staffed and in the middle of tourist season." Abigail did not look pleased about this situation.

Bree looked the woman directly in the eye, hoping she was conveying confidence as she answered, "I could start immediately if that helps. I'm also looking for a place to stay. Your brother mentioned you might be able to help with that as well. I would be really grateful for any leads you might have."

She held her breath as the woman eyed her up and down. Bree felt sure she could see right into her soul, and she wasn't sure if that was a good thing or not.

Abigail gave a nod of her head and said, "I think I can. Follow me." She stood quickly and headed down a short hallway.

Bree hurried to keep up. Could it really be that easy? Maybe God was going to help her after all. She didn't think after all this time He would even listen to her anymore, but maybe she was wrong.

FOUR

Drew Grant smiled while he drove another screw into place. He was thinking back to the walk he had taken with Kate last night on the beach. His fiancée. His smile widened at the thought. He was getting married and soon.

It was hard to believe only a year ago he had no idea Kate Winters even existed and now he was going to make her his wife. His wife. He began to whistle to express the happiness welling inside him at the thought of his upcoming wedding.

"Young man, you need to focus more on what you are doing rather than daydreaming!" The sharp voice cut quickly into Drew's thoughts as he turned to look at Agnes Johnson.

Mrs. Johnson, as she preferred to be called, thought she had VIP presence in the town because her late husband once served a single term as mayor. It was so long ago few recalled Mr. Johnson. Mrs. Johnson remembered though, and she made sure everyone else did as well.

"Sorry, Mrs. Johnson. Just thinking about my girl. It won't happen again." Drew grinned at Mrs. Johnson. He knew it was a white lie. There was no way he could not think of Kate, every hour of every day.

"Be that as it may, aren't you behind schedule? Where is that helper of yours? Why are you working alone today?"

"We're right on schedule, ma'am, just like I promised. And Lucas is working his police job today. He'll be in with me tomorrow."

"Humph! I won't be paying you anything extra if you get behind. That will be on you, young man!"

"Certainly, Mrs. Johnson. But I promised you we'd be finished next week, and we will be."

Mrs. Johnson didn't even answer him. She just turned on her heel and marched back into her house. Drew shook his head and laughed. There really was no pleasing the woman.

He'd almost turned down the job, but he'd known it wouldn't take long. The old woman was hard to please. He doubted any other contractor or handyman within fifty miles would have taken on the project.

It wasn't a difficult build either. She wanted a small, screened porch added to the back of her Cape Cod style home. As she put it, "I'm sick to death of not being able to enjoy spring because of the infernal black flies."

He could have easily handled the tiny porch addition himself, but he enjoyed working with Lucas. Besides, his little brother needed to learn how to deal with people like Mrs. Johnson if he planned to stick around.

The smile slipped off Drew's face. He had been praying for his brother daily since he'd heard about Antonio's death. He knew Lucas was still struggling with losing his partner. He hadn't known how badly though until Lucas arrived and moved in. Drew was glad he was there to help Lucas work through the pain.

It wasn't just Antonio's death either. Lucas was also struggling with relationships no thanks to his ex-fiancée. Jillian had messed with his head. Drew was also been praying for his brother to heal from her betrayal.

They spent many nights talking about it. All of it. Especially the nights when Lucas couldn't sleep. Occasionally they even called their brother, Peter, over to join them.

The brothers grew up in Florida. Over the last five years, each brother relocated to Haven. They often spent summers here when they were younger. They all loved the area so much all three had eventually moved.

Peter arrived first to pastor the small stone church in town. Drew followed shortly after and now Lucas. It was good to be together again, to have family close.

Drew would be marrying Kate soon and she would be moving into his cottage located on the edge of town. Lucas would be moving out and taking over the lease to Kate's apartment.

Drew picked up another screw and drove it into the plank as he continued adding boards to the new porch floor. Lucas would join him tomorrow and they would begin to add the overhead supports and the roof.

He continued working as his thoughts again drifted back to Kate. He began to whistle to himself. He was the happiest man alive. He was sure of it.

FIVE

Sabrina gave a gasp and sat bolt upright. She couldn't remember where she was. Thoughts tumbled through her mind as she tried to place the room.

She sank back against the pillow. Haven. She was in Haven. She was starting over. Her mind began to reel with thoughts. So much for going back to sleep now.

The last twenty-four hours had been a whirlwind of activity. She was having a hard time keeping up. She was now working as a waitress at the Three Cats Café. She was sure Abigail would reject her given how little experience she had, but instead she was readily accepted.

Abigail had then consulted with her two sisters about area rentals. They'd given her the lead on the small apartment she now occupied.

It was a cozy one bedroom over the garage of one of their neighbors. They called him "My Goodness Bert." Sabrina thought it an unusual nickname until she met him.

"Well, my goodness, I'd be happy to have you live in my apartment, my goodness."

Bert Hill was an older gentleman. His grandson had lived in the apartment above his garage until the week before. He'd headed south to Boston for an early program in engineering at MIT. Bert was happy to help a "damsel in distress." He was a character for sure.

The apartment was furnished with yard sale castoffs, but it was comfortable enough. There was a beachy theme underlying it all with lots of blues and whites spread throughout. She admired the scattering of sand dollars on the windowsills.

"I like to collect them, my goodness. I have so many they are starting to spill over everywhere. I gave some to my grandson." Bert seemed almost bashful at the admission. Bree found it endearing.

She had few possessions with her. There hadn't been time to pack everything. She would need to go shopping soon for some essentials, but for now she needed to save every penny to get her car fixed.

Bert had brought her to her car last night in his truck so she could retrieve her things. The Ritz brothers told her the car would need a new radiator as well as new brakes and some rust repaired before her inspection sticker ran out at the end of the month. They'd also recommended new tires before winter. The price they quoted for everything would wipe out what little money she had saved.

The cost shouldn't have been such an issue, but she had been foolish and naïve. She shook her head at her own gullibility.

She needed to start facing it all, including saying his name, even if it was only in her head. She knew it would be the only way he would stop having control over her. She would no longer allow him to control even her mind and thoughts.

Bryce had persuaded her to invest in a new piece of property, just on the market. He convinced her how it would be an excellent opportunity to learn more about the commercial side of real estate, especially if she wanted to become an agent one day. He was very persuasive. She'd gone to the bank that day and drained her savings account.

Between moving into a new apartment, even with the inexpensive rent Bert was asking, and the car repairs, Bree would have little left over. There was nothing she could do about it now but work harder.

The only problem was that the wages from a part-time job at the café would be minimal. She could only hope she'd make more in tips to get her car fixed quickly.

She couldn't believe how things were falling into place even with the car issues. It all started with her car breaking down right in front of the garage. Then finding a job and a place to stay, all within a short time of arriving in Haven.

She gave a slight jump as she heard a scraping noise against the window. She stepped quickly out of bed and hurried over. Standing to one side, she slowly pulled back the curtain, making sure she couldn't be seen from the street. She let out a breath she hadn't realized she was holding.

There was an apple tree outside the window and one of its branches had grown large enough that it was scraping the window slightly when the breeze blew. The branch moved over the glass, making little screeching noises every so often.

She raised a trembling hand to her head. She was being foolish. She never used to jump at small noises. She hated these anxious feelings that seemed to have taken over. She wanted to be the strong and confident woman she used to be, but she didn't know how to get back there.

She tried to remember if she'd ever mentioned Maine or Haven at any point in her conversations in Connecticut. She didn't think so. She had to believe Bryce didn't know, and he wouldn't figure out where she had gone.

Shaking off the thoughts, she grabbed clothes and stepped across the hall to the bathroom to get ready for the day. There was no use going back to sleep now. She was going to focus on the future and stop looking over her shoulder. She stood with arms braced on the counter and gave a firm nod at herself in the mirror. As the bathroom filled with steam, she tried not to let the doubts at the back of her mind have their way.

Soon Bree hurried down the street towards the Three Cats Café for her first day of work. She didn't want to appear weak or insecure. This was her chance to start over. She was tired of feeling scared.

Bryce had always made her feel inadequate, like a failure, even stupid. She needed to start acting confident again. Fake it until you make it. She thought that would be her new motto.

How hard could it be, after all, she thought to herself as she hurried down the sidewalk. *It's just getting people their food. I can do that.*

SIX

Lucas pulled his cruiser into his usual parking spot in front of the Three Cat Café. He put the vehicle in park and stretched with a loud yawn. He had a hard time getting up on the days he didn't work with Drew. It made it harder to get anything to eat before leaving for work.

The granola bar he'd snagged this morning was fading fast. He was looking forward to a cup of steaming hot coffee and whatever pastry Brenda had whipped up for today. That woman sure could cook.

The bell over the door jingled as he stepped inside. The atmosphere was off. There was no ambient background noise. He quickly scanned the room to see what was out of place.

He noticed the two men in the back booth wearing Florida hats. They were likely from out of town. A little boy sat at the counter looking upset. Lucas quickly checked out the adults with him. The boy was the spitting image of his dad, no worries there.

Lucas took in Agnes Johnson standing near the register going toe-to-toe with Colleen. Ahhh, that was the problem. A new waitress stood nearby, red-faced and looking mortified.

It seemed Mrs. Johnson was on one of her rampages. He stood and waited to see if Colleen needed his help. He really didn't want to have to arrest Mrs. Johnson for disorderly conduct.

*****

Bree glanced up when she heard the bell over the door jingle. Who else was going to witness her utter humiliation? She couldn't have been more wrong about waitressing. She'd been messing up orders all morning. It seemed she was destined to be a screw up.

Everyone had been gracious until this old woman had come in. She'd been yelling at Colleen for the last ten minutes. Everybody was staring. It was like a nightmare she couldn't wake up from.

A police officer entered and now just stood with his feet braced slightly and his hands on his belt. He was even smiling. *Great,* she thought sarcastically to herself, *he must think this is all funny. Fantastic.*

Bree braved another quick look at the officer. He didn't look that old, close to her own age. He had brown hair cut short and close but enough to run your fingers through. Um, well, if one wanted to do that of course. She felt her blush deepen.

She hadn't thought she could get any redder. Apparently, she could. She was thankful everyone would think it was because of the dressing down she was getting and not the fact that she thought the cop was cute.

She glanced at him again. She stiffened slightly as their eyes met briefly. Great, now he would think she was checking him out. A small voice reminded her she *was* checking him out.

"Anything I can help with, ladies?" His deep voice washed over her. She'd always had a thing for men with deep voices.

"Everything's fine, Lucas. Thank you. Mrs. Johnson was just letting me know how subpar her service was today and I was trying to tell her I was going to comp her meal."

"That is the *least* you could do after this incompetent waitress spilled coffee on my best slacks. I'm not sure how the stain will ever come out."

"Mrs. Johnson, I already told you we would pay to clean or replace your pants. Just give us the receipt when you decide what to do and we will happily reimburse you. This is Bree's first day on the job. She's doing her best, aren't you?"

"Yes, ma'am." Bree's voice squeaked out and she cleared her throat before she continued, "I'm so sorry, ma'am. It won't happen again. I promise."

Bree still couldn't believe how angry the woman had become over the small amount of coffee that had spilled. It wasn't even been Bree's fault. This time at least.

Just as she'd started to place the cup of coffee on the table, Mrs. Johnson spun around and hit Bree's elbow. Bree managed to save the cup from dumping all over the woman, but a small amount spilled onto Mrs. Johnson's lap. You would have to squint to see the spot she was raising such a fuss about.

"It certainly won't happen again. If you ladies have any sense, you'll fire this one and cut your losses."

Giving a loud sniff, she turned on her heel and started towards the door. The cop stepped quickly forward and opened it for her. "Ma'am, you have a nice day now."

Mrs. Johnson shot the man a look. Then she again loudly sniffed and snapped her head up as she marched out.

The entire atmosphere in the café lightened once the door closed behind her. The patrons, deciding the show was over, went back to their own meals. A hum of conversation started back up.

"Well then, what can I get for you, Lucas? Brenda made some really yummy apple muffins this morning. How about one of those and a cup of coffee?" Colleen smiled as she headed towards the kitchen.

"Sounds perfect. I'm going to grab my spot at the counter. I'd like a break from my cruiser."

"Absolutely. Bree will bring it right over."

Bree turned and hurried off to the kitchen before serving the man. She needed a moment for her face to cool before she served the handsome officer, who had just witnessed her humiliation at the hands of Mrs. Johnson.

"Welcome to Haven." Bree looked at Brenda who smiled as Bree plated a muffin fresh from the oven. "Don't mind Agnes Johnson. She's a lonely old woman who likes to make everyone as miserable as she is."

"Does she do that a lot?" Bree poured the coffee into a mug and grabbed a set of creamers and sugars to add to the tray.

"About once a week. I can't remember the last time she's actually paid for a meal. There is always something wrong and we always end up comping it."

"Great." Bree took a moment to take a few deep breaths. She grabbed her water bottle for a couple quick sips to give herself some more time to compose herself. The cop was going to have to wait a few more seconds.

"Who's the muffin for?" Brenda turned to continue rolling out the pie crust she was working on.

"I don't know. Some cop who came in just as Mrs. Johnson was demanding Colleen fire me on the spot." Bree swallowed before she choked. "Um, I do still have a job, don't I?"

"Of course, you do. We're certainly not going to fire you on your first day and especially not because Agnes demanded it."

Abigail walked into the kitchen and heard the last comment. "Don't let her bother you."

"I'll try and thank you." Bree smiled at Abigail. She was starting to like these sisters. She turned to look at Brenda as she picked back up on the conversation.

"That must be Lucas. He's such a sweet boy. Just moved here last year from Miami. He stops by a couple times a week when he's on duty." Brenda continued working on the pie.

Bree took a deep breath and grabbed the tray. She concentrated on holding it securely. She wasn't confident enough to hold it in one hand just yet and so far, she hadn't needed to. It was later in the morning and the café didn't have a lot of people. There was plenty of room to move around all morning. She wasn't sure what she would do when that wasn't the case.

Bree gave Lucas a slight smile as she unloaded the tray carefully in front of him. "Here you go. Can I get you anything else?"

"How about your name?" Lucas blinked. Had he just said that out loud? He'd been thinking it as he watched her approach. He thought the slight blush now staining her cheeks was adorable. It had been a while since he'd flirted with a cute girl. He smiled wider.

"Oh, sorry. I'm Sabrina. I'll be serving you today."

"I thought I heard Colleen call you Bree."

Why had he asked her name then? Bree wasn't sure what kind of game he was up to, but she wasn't in the mood to play it today.

"It's my nickname. Can I get you anything else?" She dropped the smile, tucked the tray under and arm, and raised an eyebrow at him.

He smiled back. "I'm good. Thanks." He dropped his eyes to the plate and didn't have the heart to tell her he'd wanted the apple muffin and not the blueberry. He looked up and gave her a wide grin. "See you around, Bree."

Bree gave a small huff of breath and headed out to make the rounds of her customers, coffee carafe held tight. What was all that about her name? And why had he grinned at her that way before she left? She'd brought him his muffin and coffee, just like Colleen had asked her to do.

Her smile faded. She'd brought the wrong muffin. She stopped and looked back over her shoulder at him. Lucas was happily eating the muffin and drinking his coffee. He caught her eye and nodded at her, smiling with his mouth closed since she caught him mid-bite.

He didn't seem to mind the mix up. Maybe she should beg Abigail to let her do something else. Bake? No, she couldn't bake. She hated baking. Maybe she should find something else. There must be some other job here in this little town she was more qualified to do. Waitressing was not going to be her thing. She could tell.

SEVEN

P eter Grant rubbed a hand down his face. The church yard sale was coming up and it seemed the women on the committee needed to ask his opinion on everything. He'd never met more dependent women in his life.

He sighed as he leaned back in his chair. It wasn't their fault. The former pastor had apparently done quite a bit of handholding. From all accounts, he'd been a bit of a control freak. Peter was the exact opposite. He preferred to only be bothered with the big questions. And the church yard sale wasn't a big question in his mind.

The women running the yard sale had been doing it for twenty or more years at this point. He'd only been their pastor for the last three. He trusted they knew a lot more about where to set up the booths, how much to charge for lemonade, and answers to the host of other questions they had been bugging him with nonstop for the last few days.

He hit the power button on his laptop and waited for it to boot up. He was seriously behind on his sermon prep. He needed to stay focused if he was going to finish it in time for Sunday. He'd spent the day chasing down tables and chairs and a host of other things for the yard sale. Now, here it was, Wednesday night, and he barely had an outline.

"Lord, I could use a little help. Can you run some interference for me, please? Better yet, can you give me the words you want me to say? How about you write this one for me? Could you do that, Lord? I'd appreciate it."

He bowed his head and continued talking to God about what it was He might want him to say. Peter was so caught up in practical church matters that he was neglecting the spiritual ones.

A soft chime sounded. Sighing, he gave a hasty "amen." Someone was in the sanctuary. So much for a quiet night, but the chime meant someone had come in through the front doors. He must have forgotten to lock them since he was still working. Figures. The interruption was not going to help him get his sermon written.

"Okay, Lord, but I'm not kidding now. You're going to have to write this one for me if You insist on sending souls my way."

Pushing the door open to the sanctuary, he looked around to see who had triggered the door alert. He still hadn't told anyone he'd installed it soon after arriving once he realized how often people showed up in the sanctuary. They all thought he had a spiritual "Spidey-sense" and he let it slide. He probably should rectify that.

"Peter! Someday you're going to have to tell me how you always know I'm here." His future sister-in-law and former foster sister, Kate Winters, smiled as she looked up from where she was sitting in the sanctuary.

49

When Kate was younger, she'd once lived as a foster child with Peter's family for several years before her father came back into her life and whisked her away. She'd lived through much abuse and neglect but had finally found healing and forgiveness just last year.

I really should confess about the door alarm he thought as he felt a slight blush cover his face. "What's up Kate? Shouldn't you be home prepping for a wedding?" He smiled with fondness as he took a seat in front of her, turning so he could talk.

"I saw the lights on and figured you were working late. I thought I'd slip in and sit for a bit, for old time's sake."

They exchanged a smile as they both remembered how often Kate used to come to the church just like this. Before they figured out their shared past, Peter was simply been a pastor sharing the Bible stories from the stained-glass windows in the sanctuary.

"You know, I don't think you ever did finish telling me all the stories." Kate grinned at him. "I think you owe me a few more."

"Are you doing okay, Kate?" Peter gave her a look of concern. He remembered how much she once struggled with anxiety.

Kate gave a small sigh. "Yeah. I just felt the need to come in tonight to sit for a bit. Things really are going well. Drew is as fabulous as always. Things are slowly getting better all the time with my dad. Life really is good. I just need a little reminder every now and then."

"You know, I was just reading this morning in the Psalms and God impressed a verse on me. I think it may have been for you."

"Oh? What does that even mean? 'Impressed on you?' How does that work?"

"Sometimes when I'm reading my Bible, God will make a verse almost jump off the page at me. Something about it will strike a chord. Or He may bring a person's name or face to mind as I'm reading. Then I know I need to pay attention."

"Huh, I never thought about it like that, but yeah, I've had that happen, too."

"This morning this verse spoke to me and maybe it's for you. It was Psalm 34:4 and it says, 'I sought the LORD, and He answered me, And delivered me from all my fears.' Give your fears to Him, Kate. Stop hanging on to them and trying to fix them. He can handle them."

Peter watched as Kate sat and stared at the front of the church where a large tapestry of Christ on the cross hung next to the pulpit. He knew she'd worked hard over the last year to release the fears which had held her back.

Kate turned and smiled at her soon to be brother-in-law. "Thanks, Peter. That's just what I needed to hear. You're right. I was starting to take back some of the things I had given over to Christ. I needed that reminder."

"Anytime. You know you can always ask me anything. And talk to Drew too, Kate. He can also help you. But more importantly, talk to God. Always take your fears and anxieties to

Him first. He can handle them far better than either Drew or I could do for you."

The two rose and embraced. "You really are a great brother. Thanks." Kate gave him a peck on the cheek and turned. "I'm going to head home. See you later, Peter."

"Have a good night, Kate." He watched her exit and then headed back to his office.

"Thanks, Lord. It seems maybe this week I'm going to talk about fear. I got the message loud and clear just now. Thank you for providing once again."

EIGHT

Bree suppressed a yawn. She hadn't been sleeping well for a while and it was beginning to affect her. She spent most of her days hyped up on coffee just to function.

She was trying to figure out how to pay for her car repairs. The repair job would wipe out what little she had in savings and she wasn't comfortable doing that at this point. Not when she didn't know how stable life would end up being.

Bree's mind continued to whirl potential fixes as she stepped out her front door on to the small deck at the top of the stairs. She pulled the door closed behind her and then double checked to make sure it was locked. Haven seemed like a safe place, and she knew many people here probably didn't lock their doors, but she had lived in the city too long to leave her apartment door open to anyone. She headed down the outside staircase to go to work.

"Well, my goodness, good morning to you, Bree. How are you doing on this fine day, my goodness?"

Bree jumped at the sound of Bert's voice. "Hi, Bert. I didn't see you there. I'm good. How are you?" Bree really didn't have time to have a long conversation this morning, but she didn't want to be rude.

"My goodness, the Lord has blessed me as always. You have a good day now."

Bree waved and smiled as she continued on her way, leaving Bert to go back to his gardening. The old man was slowly growing on her.

Bree started out at a brisk pace, heading to the café. She started thinking over the last couple of days of work. She wondered if there was any possibility of getting a few more hours.

She knew she was still the new girl, but it wouldn't hurt to ask.

The job had started to become a little easier. Maybe the owners would let her take on more.

She grimaced slightly at that thought. It was true she was getting better, but she was still messing up at least one or two things every single shift.

She couldn't believe how the owners continued to give her chance after chance. Abigail, Brenda, and Colleen were a cut above the rest of the people she had known. There was something different about them. Not just because they kept giving her chances, but there was just something she couldn't put her finger on.

She reached the café and pushed open the door. She welcomed the burst of cool air that greeted her. She knew she would be warm by the time she started delivering orders, but right now the air conditioning felt chilly. Even for an early morning, the air outside was humid.

"You're just in time. Ryann called in sick. Her little girl has a fever." Colleen called out as she started brewing a second pot of coffee. "Can you work until closing today?"

Bree thought of the extra tips. Those would certainly help with her car issues. "Yeah. Not a problem. Let me just put stuff away, grab my apron, and I'll be right out."

Was it possible God was listening to her rambling thoughts on the way here? He still seemed too far away. Too far to see or hear her, she was sure. It had to be a coincidence, a happy one at that.

*****

Lucas parked his cruiser in front of the café. He'd wanted to get here earlier. His stomach had hoped the same, but here it was closer to lunchtime than breakfast. He was starving and prayed his radio would stay quiet long enough for him to finish his meal.

He pushed open the door and saw the usual hustle and bustle that was the Three Cats Café. He smiled. He enjoyed taking his breaks here.

57

He sat at his usual spot at the counter and turned to see who was in the café. He spotted the new waitress he'd met the other day. Bree. She was across the restaurant helping a customer.

He used the moment to really look at her. She was close to his own age of twenty-eight. *Ugh,* he thought to himself, *how did I get so close to thirty?* Shaking off thoughts of his age, he continued to observe Bree. Her long dark brown hair was pulled up in a high ponytail.

"Enjoying the view?"

Lucas swung around to see Colleen with a steaming cup of coffee in one hand. She placed the mug down in front of him and cocked an eyebrow. He started to feel his cheeks go red. He hadn't blushed in years.

He decided to just play it cool and pretend like he hadn't just been caught staring like some dumbstruck teenager. "What's her story anyway?"

"Why don't you ask her that yourself, sweetie? She's headed this way now." With a wink, Colleen turned and headed to the other side of the café. He watched as she stopped and said something to Bree. Bree's head snapped up as she looked in his direction.

He turned hastily towards his coffee and took a quick gulp. Lucas then proceeded to choke on the too hot brew. *So much for acting cool,* he thought to himself as he continued to hack.

"Here, see if this helps." Bree placed a glass of ice water in front of Lucas.

"Thanks," Lucas managed to gasp out through his burning throat. He picked up the glass and took a cautious sip. The cool water did help to ease the stinging in his throat.

"Better?" Bree looked concerned. "Need anything else. A sippy cup maybe?" She smiled sweetly at him.

Lucas almost spit the mouthful of water out that he had just taken. Was the woman trying to kill him?

He glanced at her, still working to control his breathing and not choke, to see her watching, hands on hips.

Sipping cautiously again at the water, Lucas felt his throat continue to ease. He coughed once, twice, and then took another sip. Thankfully, Bree waited for him to respond this time.

"Thanks," he rasped out. "That helped."

"Anytime." Bree knew that Colleen was supposed to be covering the counter on this shift, but she'd asked Bree to wait on Lucas.

If she didn't know better, she would think Colleen was trying to push her towards the man. She didn't plan to fall into his arms though. She was going to learn to stand on her own two feet for once. Never again would she let a man determine her destiny.

NINE

Later that day, Bree stood just inside the kitchen at the Three Cats Café. She had already brought out the last check, and the lunch rush was starting to settle down. She counted her tips and realized she had taken in almost double what she normally would. Of course, it was only because Ryann was out today. She knew this wouldn't happen often enough. If she was going to get her car paid off quickly, she needed a way to bring in some extra money.

"Why the long face? Everything okay?" Colleen was walking towards her, heading back out to wipe down the tables and booths that had just been vacated.

"Yeah. Everything's fine. I was just trying to figure out how I was going to finish paying off my car repairs. I don't mind walking, but I'd really like it back soon."

"I thought my brothers had it all set for you. What's the problem?" Colleen gestured to Bree to follow her to the lines of booths opposite the counter. She handed Bree a cloth and the two women began cleaning as they continued their conversation.

"They did fix it. It's just that it was more than I was planning for and I'm a little short on funds." Bree felt her face heat. She hated not being able to pay her bills.

"I can ask my brothers to cut you a break," Colleen smiled as she continued to the next booth.

"Thanks, but I'll figure something out."

"Excuse me."

Bree jumped. She was so focused on her job and her issues she had forgotten Lucas was still sitting at the counter nursing a second cup of coffee. She knew she drank a lot of coffee, but Lucas seemed to live on the stuff. She had no idea how the man was going to sleep tonight with that much caffeine in his system.

"Sorry, but I couldn't help overhearing your problem. I think I can help."

Bree just stared at him. How was he going to help her? She certainly wasn't going to take any money from him. She didn't know him well enough, and he'd want something in return, especially if he was like most men. She wasn't that kind of woman.

"Help how?" Bree knew the tone of her voice held a note of sarcasm and incredulity to it, but she couldn't help herself. She had learned her lesson before, and she wasn't going to make the same mistake twice. Even if he was a cop.

Lucas couldn't help the smile that crossed his face. She certainly was feisty. He liked that. "My brother owns a handyman business. I work with him part-time. We're getting ready to redo his cottage before he gets married in a few months. He wants the outside painted and probably a room or two inside as well. Interested?"

Bree knew her mouth had dropped open. Painting? He wanted to offer her a job? A real job? She snapped her mouth closed. "How many hours?"

"As long as it takes, but probably a couple weeks of work. It's not that big of a place and both Drew and I will be helping as well. We have a paint sprayer for the big sections, but the rest will have to be done by hand. Have you ever done any painting?"

Bree shook her head. "Not really." She did a bit of artistic painting, but somehow she doubted there was any correlation between a landscape watercolor and house painting.

"It's not difficult work, but it is time consuming. Why don't you come over tomorrow and talk with Drew? We can work out the details."

Bree considered the offer. She wasn't sure she trusted this man, even if he was a police officer. What if he had something else in mind?

What if his brother was awful to work for? She could use the extra money and she knew it would fit in well with her hours at the café, but she just wasn't sure she could trust her own judgment on this.

It was easy to keep a distance at the café, keep it casual. But working at his brother's house would be in closer proximity. Did she want to put herself in that situation? She wasn't sure. She just knew she needed a way to earn some extra money and the offer had pretty much fallen into her lap.

"Ryann called and said her daughter is already feeling better. Why don't you plan to be done just after lunch tomorrow, Bree?" Colleen smiled as she took the bucket of soapy water to the next booth. "That should still give you plenty of time to go out and see Lucas and Drew about the painting. We can work your hours here to accommodate it easily enough."

"Are you sure?" Bree looked at Lucas and then back at Colleen.

"It'll be fine. I'm sure Ryann won't mind a couple extra hours to make up for today." Colleen walked closer and whispered for Bree's ears only, "You can trust the Grant boys." Colleen touched Bree on the arm and went back to wiping down the next booth and benches.

"Here," Lucas grabbed a small notebook from his pocket as well as a pen. "This is the address and my cell number. Call me if you change your mind. Otherwise, I'll see you there around one tomorrow."

He ripped off the paper and handed it to Bree. She took it and looked down. "How far is this from here?"

"About a ten minute drive. Not far."

"You forget, Lucas dear. She doesn't have a car right now. Why don't you plan to pick her up here and drive her out?" Colleen looked up from where she was working and winked at Lucas.

Bree felt her face flame at that suggestion and the wink. What was Colleen playing at? She might trust the Grant boys, including the one sitting right in front of Bree, but that didn't mean Bree did. Not yet anyway. "You don't have to do that. I can walk. It doesn't sound far at all."

"Sweetie, it would take you over an hour to walk that far. Let the man pick you up." She picked up the bucket, plucked the rag from Bree's limp hand, and headed back to the kitchen. "He's a good one. Just trust me."

"See you here at one tomorrow?" Lucas smiled. He was intrigued by Bree in a way he hadn't been by any woman in a long time.

Bree looked at Lucas who stood near the counter looking far more handsome than anyone should in his police uniform. She felt her stomach give a little flip and knew she was in trouble even as she gave a nod. So much trouble.

TEN

In keeping with her new start, Bree found herself in the back row of a little stone church that Sunday. She had discovered it on one of her walks to work. She still felt far from God, but maybe this would help bridge the gap.

She suppressed another yawn and wished she'd thought to bring an iced coffee with her. She struggled to keep her eyes open. She could use another dose of caffeine. It wasn't that the preacher was boring, she was just tired.

It also didn't help that the church had no air conditioning. It was one of those sweltering summer days. Even with ceiling fans turned on high, there was little relief from the hot air pressing against warm bodies.

Bree squirmed slightly to try to maneuver a little space between her and the people on either side. She felt a little claustrophobic crunched between them as well as a little extra melted from the body heat emanating from the people sitting next to her being squished together on the long pew.

She took the bulletin she had been handed when she'd walked in and, taking a cue from those nearby, began to fan herself. She wondered why the church didn't invest in air conditioning. Granted, there weren't many hot days in the summer in Maine, but when there were, they were miserable.

She spotted the sisters from the café almost as soon as she'd walked in. They were sitting near the front with their families, at least Bree presumed they were relatives.

Bree noticed a few other faces from the café including the hostess, Rosie, and Ryann, the other waitress. It seemed many in this small town attended Seaside Chapel.

She couldn't remember the last time she had attended church. Before coming back to Haven, she rarely went. She tried to go on special occasions like Easter or Christmas, but she didn't go weekly. She didn't even go monthly for that matter.

Her work took up much of her time with the long commute into the city. She started taking the entire weekend to get errands done and have some downtime.

She remembered when she was younger how she'd gone every Sunday and loved it. She'd looked forward to the fun at Sunday School and learning about Jesus.

Some of her fondest memories were sitting in a pew, much like this one, between her grandparents. She still missed them every day.

Bree missed the fellowship of others when she first stopped going. Then it had just become more of a habit not to go. She hadn't meant to, of course. There was no pivotal moment when she decided God wasn't for her. One week turned into two and then three and before she knew it, it was months since she attended.

While she missed it on occasion at the start, it wasn't enough to give up her Sundays of sleeping in. She always planned to go back, but the weeks just started bleeding into one another. Sometimes she would feel a pull to return, but she would shove the feeling aside or hit snooze on her alarm.

She wiggled again and felt the eyes of the woman beside her glancing at her. She quickly stilled. She forced herself to tune in to what was being said from the pulpit.

"We were not given a spirit of fear."

Bree sat up straighter and looked up. She had so much fear in her lately that she was starting to have a hard time remembering what it felt like not to be afraid. She was just scared all the time.

Her thoughts were always focused on the what if or what next. What if he tracked her down? What would happen then? Did she really want to live in Haven? What if she couldn't get the car repairs paid for? What if she couldn't pay her rent? She didn't want to live in her car. She didn't even have a car to live in currently.

Bree shook off the worrying thoughts and tuned back into the pastor.

"In 2 Timothy 1:7 we read these words, 'For God has not given us a spirit of timidity, but of power and love and discipline.' Other translations have the word 'fear' in place of 'timidity.' Either way we need to remember that there is power in the living God. It is a power we have access to whenever we ask our Lord for help. He's here. Just waiting."

Could she do that? Could she trust in the Lord to help her not feel so afraid? Was it as simple as what the pastor just said? Would the Lord help her if she asked? It had been a long time since she had spoken to God or trusted Him in any way. She just wasn't sure anymore.

Then she remembered how things were lining up for her to be able to pay off her car. Lucas had picked her up at the café as planned just a couple days before and driven her out to Drew's house.

72

The little cottage was tucked cozily into a grove of pine trees on a bluff overlooking the ocean. She loved the look of the place from first glance.

The weathered board siding was grey and peeling. The white trim looked in desperate need of freshening up.

"Welcome! Lucas tells me you might be interested in a little side job helping us paint this place. Let me show you what I have in mind and then we can talk particulars."

Bree was instantly at ease with Drew. His bright smile matched his bright blond hair. Even though he towered over her - he must be well over six feet tall - she never felt intimidated by him.

"With the three of us working, it will probably take a week or so to get everything scraped, sanded, and repainted." Drew continued talking as they walked around the perimeter of the house. "The work isn't technical, just long and laborious."

"Laborious, huh?" Lucas punched his brother lightly in the arm. "You don't need to impress her with your big vocabulary, you know."

Bree's face heated slightly at the thought that anyone was trying to impress her and then realized it was just two brothers bantering. She smiled as she watched them continuing to rib each other as they made their way to a small shed near the tree line.

"Pay no attention to Lucas." Drew pointed at his brother. He then cleared his throat loudly and shot a grin at his brother before he continued, "All the supplies are in here. You can work around your schedule at the café. Plan to work the first day or two with either Lucas or me and we'll show you the ropes. After that, you can come and go as you please. Sound good?"

Bree was amazed. She'd just met the man. He asked for no references. He didn't seem to care she had zero experience.

"Sure. Sounds good. My only issue might be transportation, but it doesn't seem like a long walk."

"Oh right, that reminds me." Drew stepped further into the shed and removed a mountain bike from the wall where it was hanging on pegs. "I think the tires need a little air and the chain might need to be oiled. You're welcome to use it while you're working here. It'll make it easier to get back and forth."

Bree just stared at Drew and Lucas. Were they for real? Drew was not only hiring her, but he was loaning her a bike as well. This would never happen in the city. Ever. People there were far too suspicious.

"I haven't ridden a bike since I was a kid, but you know what they say." She'd laughed nervously at the thought of getting on the bike in front of Lucas and Drew, but now was as good of a time as any.

The men quickly made sure the tires were good and added a few squirts of oil to the chain. "I think it's ready to go if you want to try it out," Drew said as he pushed the bike towards her.

She stifled a grin at the memory. She wobbled her way along for only a few feet and then she straightened out and been able to stop and turn with ease. Apparently, it wasn't a skill one lost easily. It really was like riding a bike.

She would start the job tomorrow. She still remembered how her eyes popped when Drew told her how much he was going to pay her.

"The job is $500. That's for the outside work and helping to do a couple rooms inside. How's that sound?"

Not only would it pay off her car repair, but she'd have a little left over. If she could keep picking up extra shifts at the café, she'd be doing well.

A smile crossed Bree's face as she focused once more on the church service. Her eyes began to roam around the sanctuary. The church was beautiful. She loved the stone façade the moment she had seen it. Inside was just as gorgeous.

Four stained-glass windows lined each side of the sanctuary. There was a center row of pews with two aisles to each side of it. A row of pews ran down the side before each set of windows.

Her eyes took in the stained-glass windows. They were intricate in details. Each told a Bible story. She reached into her mind to see if she could recall any of them.

One was obviously the nativity story. There was a picture of Mary and Joseph sitting by a manger holding a baby with an angel above them. There was another with a shepherd holding a sheep over his shoulders walking down a hillside. She thought that had something to do with a flock of sheep and losing one.

Her eyes headed to the next window but stopped. She spotted Lucas sitting a few rows ahead of her on the opposite side of the aisle.

He was sitting next to Drew and a woman she didn't recognize. It must be Drew's fiancée. She didn't think Lucas had a girlfriend, but she didn't really know. She didn't know a lot about him other than he seemed to like pastries and coffee at the café, he worked part-time as a police officer, and part-time with his brother.

And Bree didn't know why the thought of Lucas having a girlfriend bothered her, because she just realized it did. She let her eyes travel once more to the preacher before finding herself again looking towards Lucas.

Now that she found where he was sitting, she couldn't seem to not look at him. Lucas was paying close attention to the pastor.

Bree glanced back to the pulpit again, but her eyes drifted right back to Lucas. He'd been funny and witty yesterday and had made her laugh more than once. She'd enjoyed their time together, more than she thought she would.

She studied his profile. He had a straight nose over a wide mouth that easily smiled. His eyes were guarded though. She thought it must have something to do with his job. She was sure he had seen things she'd never understand. Well, maybe not in Haven, but hadn't she heard someone mention how he once lived in Miami?

He had a head of thick, dark brown hair. She'd always liked dark haired men. She shook her head slightly. No, she wasn't even going to go there.

No matter how much fun she'd had with him yesterday, she remembered her vow not to rely on a man again. She needed to figure out her own life before she invited anyone else in. And she wasn't sure she ever wanted that. It seemed safer to swear off men all together. Less hassle. Less pain.

Just then Lucas turned slightly and looked back at her, catching her staring at him. A blush stained her cheeks as she saw him smile and wink at her before looking forward again.

Great, just great, Bree, she thought to herself. Now what was she going to do about that?

ELEVEN

Lucas smiled to himself. He enjoyed not being on the receiving end of one of Mrs. Johnson's tirades. She seemed to be in rare form today.

"Young man! What are you smiling at over there? Pay attention to what you are doing and get busy. I have never seen two lazier men in my entire life."

Lucas felt the smile slide off his face. He turned and grabbed a handful of shingles and started nailing them in place. He listened as his brother worked to placate the old biddy.

"Now, now, Mrs. Johnson, if you keep giving us such compliments are heads are going to swell." Drew shot her his most charming grin as he snagged a nail and hammered it into place.

Drew and Lucas were working on finishing up the roof of the little porch they were adding to Mrs. Johnson's house. Lucas could tell Drew was having to use all his charm today. He wasn't sure what had Mrs. Johnson in a tizzy but she was upping her game.

Lucas caught his brother's eye and made sure Mrs. Johnson couldn't see his face before rolling his own eyes. If Lucas didn't love his brother so much, he would never have agreed to continue working on this job. The woman was beyond insufferable.

"Why don't you go have a cup of tea, Mrs. Johnson? It will be much quieter inside and then Lucas and I can focus on the job. You can come out at lunchtime and inspect. Give us a chance to finish up without distraction."

With a loud huff, the old woman turned on her heel and marched inside. Lucas was always amazed at how well his brother managed to derail the woman's diatribes.

"That really is remarkable you know." Lucas shot a grin at his brother as silence

81

descended around them. They could hear the birds start to chirp once more. It seemed even they were afraid of Mrs. Johnson.

"It's just my natural charm, bro."

"I think most of the town folks would disagree with you. For some odd reason, you're the only person I have ever seen who can get her to stop mid-tirade and walk away like that. It's a sight to behold. I'm pretty sure half the town is jealous of your talent."

Drew laughed as he grabbed another shingle. He shot a glance at his brother. "How are things going these days? Anything new and exciting on the police front?"

"Let's see. I wrote a ticket the other day for someone who decided to do a U-turn on Main Street and cut off Mrs. Johnson."

"Yikes."

"Yeah, that was fun. I would have normally given the poor dude a warning, but, well, it was Mrs. Johnson. She wanted me to toss him in jail for twenty-four hours to 'cool his heels' as she said. I wrote the ticket as quickly as I could while she stood there telling me what I should be doing differently. I'm pretty sure the guy thanked me about twenty times before he escaped."

Drew laughed as he continued rhythmically nailing down the new shingles. They were on schedule to complete the roof today. That would leave Drew to finish the project tomorrow with all the small finishes and then clean up. Right on schedule as he had promised.

After that, he could focus on his own place. In just a few short months, Drew would be a husband. A grin slowly spread across his face.

"You know I can always tell when you're thinking about Kate, right?"

"What?" Drew looked at his brother with a quizzical look.

"You get a silly grin on your face every single time. Every time, man."

"I have no idea what you're talking about."

Lucas laughed. "Yeah, right." He grabbed some more nails and shingles and began working his way towards his brother.

"Fine. Okay. I was thinking about Kate. Shoot me. I'm going to be married soon, and I can't wait."

The two men fell into a companionable silence as they continued to work on the roof. Lucas found himself remembering catching Bree looking at him in church. He smiled as he remembered winking at her.

"Speaking of women," Drew interrupted Lucas's thoughts, "Bree seems nice. How's the painting going?"

Lucas felt his brothers eyes on him. He knew he was waiting to see how he would react. Lucas continued nailing shingles, not giving Drew the satisfaction of knowing how his heart rate had accelerated slightly or how his stomach lurched a little at the thought of spending more time with Bree.

Play it cool, man. Play it cool, Lucas thought to himself. "Not a problem. Bree is a quick learner. It's been going fine. It should be easier than dealing with you know who." He nodded towards the house.

"What's the story with you and Bree anyway?"

Lucas glanced at his brother in surprise. Drew knew all about Jillian and what had happened there. Lucas had spent time discussing it with Drew until he came to the decision he was going to swear off women for a long time. He was done feeling like an idiot and being made to look like one as well.

"Nothing. I met her at the Three Cats. I heard she needed some extra cash, so I brought her out to see about hiring her to help paint. You know how much I just love painting." Lucas made sure there was plenty of sarcasm dripping from his voice. Painting was his least favorite thing to do.

He continued, "I'm not really looking for a relationship you know. Just because you're in love doesn't mean everyone else has to be."

"If that's the case, why were you winking at her in church yesterday?"

TWELVE

Bree pedaled the bike down the road heading out of town. She was going to her first day working at Drew's house. She wondered if Lucas would be there. Would it be awkward to see him after he had winked at her in church?

Of course not, she smiled to herself. She was being silly. It didn't mean anything, she was sure. Some people just winked. Right? He was just being friendly. That was it.

She enjoyed the breeze on her face as she pumped her legs. Thankfully, there weren't a lot of hills on the way to Drew's cottage although the road had a few sharp turns in it. She stayed as close as she could to the side of the road without leaving the hard surface. She was still working to feel comfortable on the bike.

Drew assured her he would have all the tools she needed. She just needed to show up. She tucked a water bottle and a peanut butter and jelly sandwich in a backpack along with some sunscreen and a few granola bars.

Bree wore her oldest pair of jeans. They were worn thin around her knees and back pockets but still held fast – barely. She wore a loose white t-shirt with a few holes in the hem. Over this she had on a flannel shirt from Bert.

When she'd mentioned she would be biking out to Drew's to paint, he handed her his "favorite painting shirt." She didn't have the heart to decline, so she had taken it. She now had it on with the sleeves rolled up and the hem tied around her waist. It was keeping her warm during the cool morning.

Bree's hair was pulled up in a ponytail with the tail tucked through the opening at the back of a ball cap, also provided by Bert. "Best to keep paint out of your hair, my goodness. It's a bear to get out, my goodness, once it gets in there."

She pulled into Drew's driveway and didn't see Lucas's truck parked anywhere. He must be working his police job today. That meant it would probably be Drew showing her what to do.

She was glad she had tucked her earbuds into her pack as well. She had started listening to a podcast about creating boundaries in your life. Maybe it would help her get things straightened out. Maybe.

Jumping off the bike, she leaned it against the shed where Drew had said the supplies would be kept. She heard rustling noises inside and tentatively called out, "Hello?"

Drew's blonde head poked out the doorway. "Hi there! Morning. Right on time. I was just digging out the scrapers and a stepladder. Take these."

He thrust a hand towards Bree, and she grabbed the scrapers and pushed the door open wider. "Let me grab the ladder. I need to head out soon to go finish another project. Lucas will be showing you what to do. Head on over the front of the house and I'll be right behind you."

Bree did as she was told, snagging her backpack from where she'd dropped it on the ground. If Lucas was going to be showing her what to do, that must mean he was around here somewhere.

She took a moment to look out at the ocean. There were small breakers forming just offshore. She closed her eyes, lifted her face to the sun, and breathed deeply.

"Best part about living here." She jumped as she heard Drew speaking behind her.

"I bet. Sorry about that. I won't let myself get distracted. I promise."

"No worries. I hope you'll enjoy it while you're here. Feel free to walk down to the beach on breaks. The path is just over there." Drew pointed with his free hand. He had a large stepladder clasped in his other.

Drew leaned the ladder against the house. Then laid out all the supplies. Once done, Drew turned and said, "Feel free to come and go without knocking. Bathroom is just down the hall. Water bottles are in the fridge, help yourself. Lucas should be along shortly. If you want to start scraping, it's pretty easy." Drew grabbed the right tool and gave a few quick swipes on the boards.

"Do your best to get it as smooth as you can, nothing left popping up and it should be fine."

"Thanks." Bree smiled at him and watched him walk into the house. She then inserted her ear buds, tapped the podcast to play, and started working.

*****

Lucas pulled on a long sleeve t-shirt before heading out the door. He couldn't wait to get his truck back from the shop. The brakes had started squealing the other day. Drew would be taking him back into town this afternoon to pick it up.

He rounded the corner of the house and found Bree hard at work. She was working her way down the side of the house as far as she could reach without the ladder. He watched as she stretched on her toes to work a stubborn spot.

Lucas cleared his throat and started towards Bree. He knew he needed to make himself known and get to work. He had been enjoying watching her, but he wasn't sure if she would appreciate the attention.

"Morning, Bree."

Bree kept on working without acknowledging she had heard Lucas's greeting. Was she mad about the wink? That was ridiculous. It was only a wink.

Lucas knew the possibility was there. After all, he had grown up with three sisters. He understood how fast they could get mad and how minor the infractions could be to make them so.

"Uh, Bree? Everything okay?" He called again as he made his way slowly closer.

Still no response.

Lucas reached out a tentative hand and tapped Bree's shoulder.

She let out a scream and threw a fist out and around as she jumped back. Her hat flew off her head and the paint scraper she was holding went flipping end over end towards the woods.

Lucas ducked reflexively and felt Bree's fist brush his shoulder.

"Lucas!" Bree placed a hand over her wildly beating heart. "You scared me!"

"Obviously," Lucas replied dryly. "Remind me not to do that again." He smiled at her. "Morning."

Bree scooped her hat off the ground and looked around for her paint scraper. She finally saw it ten feet behind where she was standing and went to fetch it.

"Why didn't you call out to me or something?"

Lucas shook his head with a wry grin on his face. "I did. Twice."

"Oh." Bree wiped her hands on the front of her pants and took a few deep breaths to try to get her heart under control. "I guess I didn't hear you."

Lucas just laughed. "That's good to know. I'd be worried if that's how you greet everyone normally."

"No, I was listening to a podcast and was really focused on what they were saying. Sorry." She smiled sheepishly.

"Mind if I work beside you?" Lucas thought it best to let her call the shots. Something was off and not just because of the way she had just acted. It felt like she had a large wall built up. He didn't want to scare her away before he even really got to know her.

"Sure." Bree shrugged as if she didn't care what he did.

Lucas was hoping that wasn't the case, but he had all day to find out. A grin spread across his face as he went to grab a scraper. He was going to enjoy finding out just how he affected Bree Martin.

THIRTEEN

Stepping back from where she was working, Bree arched backwards to stretch. She had been working for the last few hours and was starting to get sore.

She thought waitressing was tiring, but that was nothing compared to this. She could barely lift her arms and it had only been a few hours on the first day. She wasn't sure how she was going to survive a few weeks of this. Then she reminded herself of what the result would be, money to get her car back.

"Want to take a break for lunch?"

Bree jumped. She was so caught up in her thoughts of how much her body hurt, she hadn't heard Lucas get off the ladder and walk around the corner where he had been working. She needed to stop jumping every time the man spoke to her.

Lucas chuckled. "Sorry. I didn't mean to scare you. Again."

"I was just lost in my thoughts about how sore I am." She pulled a face as she rotated both shoulders back, trying to stretch them.

"Sounds like a good time to take a break then. C'mon."

Bree stood still for a moment. Lunch. She hadn't realized she was hungry until Lucas mentioned it. This was different than the café though. This was in his house. Almost like a date.

She shook her head. That was ridiculous. This was in no way a date. It was co-workers eating lunch together. It happened all over the place every single day.

Bree started towards Lucas, snagging her backpack as she went. She unzipped it as she walked, tucked her phone and earbuds inside, and then slung it over one shoulder.

"After you," Lucas said as he pulled open the door and stepped back to let Bree walk in front of him.

Bree had only been in once so far and that was for a quick bathroom trip. She hadn't really looked around. She hadn't wanted to get caught snooping.

The cottage was cozy. They were standing in the living room, which opened to a small kitchen tucked off to one side. She knew the short hallway led to the bathroom and a couple of bedrooms, which she couldn't help but notice earlier. The furnishings were oversized and worn.

"We have sandwich fixings. Do you prefer turkey, ham, or BLT? I think there's some leftover bacon from breakfast." Lucas glanced over one shoulder as he stood in front of the open door to the fridge.

"I brought a peanut butter and jelly sandwich with me. I can eat that."

"Are you sure? We have plenty here."

Bree was feeling a bit reluctant to share Lucas's food. Somehow that made it feel more date-like, but she really didn't like peanut butter and jelly either. It was all she'd had available this morning though.

"Okay. A BLT would be wonderful. Thanks."

Lucas pulled a head of lettuce from the fridge. "Can you wash this? I'll get busy on the rest."

Bree took the lettuce and went to the sink. She tried to think of something to talk about. Anything. She'd never been good at casual small talk though.

"What do you think of all this?" Lucas waved a knife around, almost like he was conducting an unseen orchestra. "My brother needs some help in here I think."

"It's cute." Bree glanced at Lucas who was slicing the tomato he had rummaged from the fridge.

"Cute? That isn't the first word that comes to mind. Frat cast offs is more like it. Thankfully, Kate has a sense of style, even though my brother does not. We're going to be working on updating everything before their wedding. It's going to be a tight deadline."

"I'm sure it will be wonderful by the time you're done. Do you know which rooms he wanted painted in here?"

"Kitchen and living room for sure." He nodded at the faded yellow color throughout. "And maybe the master bedroom. He wanted to get some input from Kate first."

"That sounds wise." Bree set the lettuce beside Lucas and grabbed a couple slices of bread to begin constructing her sandwich.

"Drew's rarely had time to work much on this place. We just tackled a porch addition for Mrs. Johnson."

"I'm sorry." Kate gave a small shudder.

"Well, I think deep down she's more bark than bite, but yeah. It was certainly an interesting time working there."

Bree took the water bottle Lucas handed her and picked up her plate. She stood awkwardly, trying to figure out what to do next.

"Let's go sit on the deck. There's a good view of the water from there and it's shaded." Lucas grabbed his own lunch and headed towards the double doors leading out to the back.

Sitting down at the small table, Bree took in the view. "This is really lovely. What a great place to live. I don't think I'll ever tire of seeing the ocean. I've never lived near water."

She quickly took a bite of her sandwich to stop her rambling. What had gotten into her? She didn't want to share too much. Not yet. No matter what Colleen had said, she still wasn't a hundred percent convinced she could trust Lucas Grant.

"I don't think I could ever live where I didn't have water nearby and preferably the ocean."

Bree took a bite of her sandwich to stall a reply. The moment her car had coughed and died in the Ritz brothers parking lot, she had known Haven was calling to her.

Bree swallowed before replying, "I can understand why. Haven is growing on me." She smiled at Lucas before taking another bite and letting her gaze drift back to the sea.

She didn't notice his return smile or how his gaze focused squarely on her.

FOURTEEN

Kate Winters hummed quietly to herself as she worked on making a necklace from a piece of sea glass she had found yesterday on her beach walk. She hadn't been this happy in years. She'd found her family, fallen in love, and found God all within the last year. Blessing upon blessing as Mama Jill would say.

She almost pinched herself to be sure it wasn't all a dream. She stopped because if it was a dream, she didn't want to wake up. Not now. Not ever. She was going to marry the love of her life in just a few months. It would also make her a Grant once and for all.

Who could have imagined she would one day be a part of the family she once thought of as hers? She had once been a foster child of the Grants years ago after her mother died, and her father abandoned her. Then, as the Grants had been preparing to adopt her, her neglectful alcoholic father suddenly came back into her life and whisked her away. She thought she'd never be part of a real family, one where she would never doubt she was loved.

Now she had a relationship with her father that was as close to normal as it could be, she was reunited with the Grants, and she would soon marry Drew, their son. A small sigh escaped as a smile crossed her face. Life really was good.

She lifted her head to take a break from the close work of threading wire around the small piece of sea glass and smiled wider as she took in her store. She had built Seascapes from the ground up and loved how it had turned out.

"Hey there, sunshine!" Her best friend and co-worker, Fiona Gillam, breezed through the front door, coffee in hand. Fiona never seemed to be without coffee.

"What's in the bag?" Kate's nose lifted as she tried to decipher what might be hidden just out of sight in the pastry bag from the Three Cats Café.

"I swung by Three Cats on the way in. Brenda was just finishing some hand pies. I snagged us a couple hot off the press, so to speak."

The two women happily munched and sipped while they caught up with what needed to be done at work that day. They had been friends almost from the time Kate arrived in Haven and opened her store.

Fiona rescued her one morning when Kate was trying to juggle a cup of coffee and her oversized purse while digging out her keys to unlock the door. Her purse slipped off her shoulder and ended up on the ground. Thankfully, her coffee had not.

Ever since that fateful meeting, Fiona had been in Kate's life. She just inserted herself and never left. Kate hadn't regretted it. There was a joy about Fiona that was contagious.

Although, now that Kate took a long look at her friend, she realized there was something off about her. Her usual joy was there but there was a sparkle missing from her eyes.

"What's up?" Kate looked at Fiona with the knowing look of a friend you can't hide anything from.

"Not a thing." Fiona gave a forced chuckle. "I'm just a little tired."

Fiona put her head down and her long curly red hair swung forward over her face. Kate could tell she was trying to hide something from her. She tried again.

"Fiona." Kate used her stern voice. She knew her friend and she knew something was off. "Tell me and tell me now. What is going on with you?"

"You don't need to worry about me, sweetie. I'm right as rain. Let's talk wedding details!"

Kate leveled a long look at her friend before conceding. "You're going to tell me. And soon. Promise?"

"There's nothing to tell, Kate. Honestly. I'm fine."

The day Fiona told her best friend what was troubling her would need to wait. She was in love with their pastor and Kate's future brother-in-law, Peter. And Peter had made it clear he wasn't going to date, and she didn't know what she was going to do about it.

FIFTEEN

Order up!" The cook yelled over the din of the café and hit the bell on the counter. Bree hurried over to grab the plates and made her way through the crowded dining room. Apparently, the summer little league championship was earlier. The Haven Hornets had taken the trophy and it seemed half the town was here celebrating with burgers and shakes.

All hands were on deck. Abigail, Colleen, and Brenda had all come back to help. Bree and Ryann had been overwhelmed as people kept pouring in. The line outside was at least fifteen people deep and every single table, booth, and stool was taken.

Bree looked up and saw a patron waving to snag her attention. She sighed as she hurried over. She was thankful for the income, but waitressing was not what she wanted to be doing. She had finally dug her camera out of one of the boxes she'd brought with her from Connecticut.

She was glad she'd grabbed it at the last minute. Bree was enjoying once more snapping photos as she walked the beach. She was reminded how much she used to love photography.

She originally moved to Connecticut to start working in the field of commercial photography. She had always been good with a camera. She had thought her skills worthy enough to try making it in a bigger area. It was why she had gone to New York City without a backwards glance. Then she found out how her skills weren't anything special. Not compared to the photographers who had been doing it for years and had all the right connections.

Instead, she ended up working in the secretary pool at a commercial real estate office to pay her bills. She'd given up her plan of being a professional photographer. Instead, she focused on working her way up to become a real estate agent. She didn't have a passion for the business, but it was a way to earn a living, and a good one at that. Over time she let her dreams die and worked to create new ones.

Now she wasn't sure what she wanted anymore, especially here in Maine. The hustle and bustle of the city had lured her at one time. Now she wondered why she had ever left Maine behind.

She could breathe easier in the country. And she was rediscovering her love of photography, of capturing moments, freezing them in time. She even planned to start sketching and drawing again. She missed being creative more than she realized.

Sighing, she continued to weave her way across the restaurant. While she was grateful for the job, she needed to figure out something else. There had to be some way she could support herself that didn't require her to stand for eight or more hours a shift. Something where she could use the creative side once more.

She wiggled her toes in her sensible black shoes. They were supposed to give "all day support." She laughed quietly. She wondered if it would ever get any easier.

*****

Lucas leaned back in the booth he was occupying at the back of the café and found his eyes tracking Bree as she hustled around, bringing orders to hungry families.

He'd noticed how she'd gotten better at keeping all the orders straight. Although, he never told her when she got his order wrong, which was still often. He smiled to himself. It seemed he had an effect on the new waitress, and he was starting to enjoy it.

It was fun working with her at Drew's as well. She was starting to relax with him, a little more each day. He could feel her barriers slowly coming down.

He smiled as he remembered yesterday. They had finally finished up all the scraping. It was tiring work and the cottage looked worse than it had when they'd started. But when they sanded all the rough spots and applied some new paint, it would look spectacular.

Bree let out a loud groan and stretched her back. "I'm beat. Who knew it took that much arm muscle to scrape a house?" She smiled tiredly at Lucas as they worked together to clean up the tools for the day.

"Can I give you a lift home?" He held his breath slightly hoping she would say yes. He continued to move slowly. He was really enjoying the woman he was getting to know. He had offered her a ride every night over the last week and she turned him down each time.

"No thanks. I can use the exercise." Bree offered the same excuse she did each night as well. "Besides, it's my arms that get the workout here. My legs are starting to feel neglected."

Lucas wasn't able to help himself as his eyes flicked over her jean encased legs. "They look good to me."

He watched as a blush covered her cheeks. She was absolutely adorable when she blushed like that.

Now she seemed to be avoiding him at the café. He hoped his comment earlier today hadn't replaced bricks in the wall he was working to break down. He had just torn down a few and hoped they would stay down.

He knew Bree usually handled the counter during the days and the booths when she worked in the evenings. Not that he was stalking her or anything. He was just observing. It was part of his job, after all.

He had taken the booth in the back corner with hopes it would be in her section. Instead, Colleen waited on him. He knew he should vacate it soon. The line outside looked like it was getting restless. He caught Colleen's eye as she hustled by. "I'll take the check whenever you have a minute."

She nodded and kept moving to the counter to pick up another order to deliver. Lucas sat back and finished off his drink.

While he usually came in for pastries, the Three Cats also did an amazing job on burgers and fries. He had treated himself to a milkshake tonight as well. He would add an extra mile or two to his run in the morning as penance.

He looked up as Bree headed his way. He was slouched trying to watch her without being seen. He straightened quickly, but it appeared he was caught after all.

"Colleen asked me to drop this off for her. Have a good night." She turned to walk away.

"Wait!" Lucas felt a slight warmth coming into his cheeks. He would *not* blush right now. What was he, fifteen again?

He cleared his throat as Bree stopped and looked back at him. "I was wondering…" His voice trailed off. He didn't remember this being so hard. Did he even want to go on a date? He looked up. Yeah, he wanted to get to know Bree better.

Bree tapped her foot impatiently. "Did you need something else? I can let Colleen know."

"No, I'm all set. Thanks."

"Okay. Have a nice night."

"Actually, there is one more thing." Lucas cleared his throat once more. "I was wondering if I could take you out some time?" He prayed as he waited to see what she would say. *Lord, let her say yes. I feel you pushing me forward. Let it be what you want most of all.*

Lucas waited. Why was it taking her so long to answer? Was that a good thing? *Lord, help me out here, please.*

"Um, I don't think that's a good idea." Bree spun abruptly on her heel and hurried back to the kitchen.

Well, that hadn't gone as he hoped, but Lucas wasn't going to let one rejection scare him off. He would have to come up with a Plan B and fast.

"Okay, Lord, the direct approach didn't work. If this is what you want, help me figure out the indirect path to take," he said under his breath as he dropped his money on the table and headed out the door. He continued mumbling to himself, "I feel you leading me.

Give me patience while I wait for you to make it clear to me what you want me to do about her."

Lucas glanced back to see Bree watching him from just inside the kitchen door. He winked at her and smiled before he thought better of it and left the café, whistling.

SIXTEEN

Bree started walking home from working at the café, her thoughts going back to Lucas asking her out. It was unexpected. She was second-guessing her decision to say no so out of hand.

The café was the busiest she had ever seen tonight. She couldn't seem to focus right now. Her feet ached. She felt a headache coming on. Life was just too confusing.

Her brain felt full of wool. It was hard to make any decisions since she was beyond tired. Her tired was tired. She covered a yawn with her hand and kept trudging ahead.

She was so wrapped up in her own misery and exhaustion she didn't notice the sound of steps behind her. She suddenly realized how vulnerable she was walking alone. How foolish could she be?

She glanced behind her and saw a man walking purposefully toward her. He was wearing a baseball cap pulled so low she couldn't see his face. His hands were tucked into the pockets of his jeans.

Bree picked up her pace as she tried to figure out what to do. She wanted to bolt for home. Bert might be there, but she wasn't sure. He liked to go bowling with his buddies a few evenings a week. It wasn't like the older man would be able to do much if someone were following her anyway.

She should go back to the café. It was closer than her apartment. But if she went back, she'd have to go right past whoever was behind her. She started looking around for people.

Where were all the people? It seemed like she usually passed at least a few people out enjoying the nice summer evenings on her walk home. Now there seemed to be no one around. Twilight had started to descend and with it, people must have headed inside.

It seemed there was nowhere to go but forward as fast as possible. She began walking as quickly as she could as she fumbled for her keys.

She pulled out her apartment key. She wanted to be able to get up the stairs and get inside fast. She was moving just short of a run now and her breath began to come out in small puffs and pants.

Bree glanced again behind her and saw the man still following. He was getting closer with each step.

Was it him? Bryce couldn't have found her. Not yet. It had only been a few weeks. She had started to feel safe. She had started to let her guard down. How could she have been so stupid?

In her haste, she felt her keys slip through her fingers and fall to the ground. She nearly tripped as she bent to scoop them up. She stood frozen. She didn't know what to do.

"Hey there, need a lift?"

Bree looked around wildly. She was in such a panic she didn't heard the old beat-up pickup pull up beside her. Lucas was leaning forward with his arm on the steering wheel peering through the passenger window at her.

"Everything okay, Bree?"

Bree turned and glanced back the way she had come but the man was gone. She turned in a circle as she looked frantically around. Where had he gone? Was it even Bryce?

She didn't hear Lucas get out of his truck and come up beside her. She screamed and threw a punch as she felt a touch on her arm. The blow glanced off Lucas's shoulder.

"Whoa!" He held up both hands. "It's just me. What's wrong?" As Lucas reached out again slowly, Bree fell into his arms and grabbed the front of his shirt in her fists. She was panting and began to cry.

"I'm sorry. I'm sorry. I didn't mean to hit you." She hung on to the safety net Lucas offered.

"It's okay. Shhhhh. You're safe." She felt him rubbing small circles on her back. She tried to catch her breath, but she couldn't seem to relax enough. "Just breathe. It's alright." She heard Lucas continue to murmur words of encouragement to her.

Bree hung on to Lucas with all her strength. She thought she was safe. How had Bryce found her? Was it even him? Was she losing her mind?

She groaned aloud. "I don't know what to do!"

Lucas gently detached himself from Bree and pushed her out to arm's length. He bent slightly at the knees to look her in the face. "Bree, look at me. I promise. You're safe. I won't let anything happen to you, but you have to tell me what's going on. I can't protect you if I don't know what's wrong."

Bree just shook her head and willed herself to stop shaking. She tried to pull herself together, but tears continued to track down her face.

"Come on, let's get in my truck and off the street."

Bree moved mechanically as Lucas opened the passenger door and helped her settle in. She sat and trembled with her face buried in her hands. She didn't even notice when he reached across her and snapped her seat belt closed and then shut the door gently.

It was too late. Bryce had found her. She would have no choice but to run. Going back wasn't an option.

SEVENTEEN

Choking back another sob, Bree worked to pull herself together. She thought she couldn't cry anymore, but just when she thought she was finished, another shot of fear would start her going again. She was tired of being afraid. All the decisions she had made in the last few months were based on that emotion.

It didn't matter though. She would have to run. That was all there was to it. She would have to go somewhere he could never find her. She had no idea how Bryce had tracked her to Haven. She hadn't even known she was coming here until her car died at the town garage.

She still wasn't sure it was even Bryce. The build looked right but he would never be caught wearing a baseball cap. He'd once told her he found them demeaning. She just wasn't certain it was him, which made it hard to decide what to do.

Bree felt Lucas wrap a blanket around her where she was sitting on his couch. He must think she was crazy at this point. She'd lashed out at him twice now after being surprised. No normal person did that.

"Here, drink this. It will help."

She felt a mug placed carefully into her hands. She automatically took a tentative sip. Chamomile tea. Maybe it would help her sleep tonight, but she doubted it. Not with the possibility that Bryce had found her.

Bree jumped sloshing tea over her pants as she heard a soft bang from the kitchen as Lucas shut the cabinet door.

"Sorry about that." Lucas walked in with his own mug of tea and handed her a towel.

"Are you ready to tell me what's going on that has you jumping at cupboard doors." Lucas sat in a nearby chair and took a sip of his drink as he waited for her to respond.

123

Bree kept her head down and mopped the tea off her slacks. She didn't look at him as she took another sip. "It was just a long day at work. It's nothing. Really. I'm just overtired." Bree tried to bring up a small smile to reassure Lucas and herself.

She began to rise and set down the mug. "I really should be going."

"Sit down. It's okay. You're safe. I'm a cop. I'm sworn to protect you, remember?"

Bree sank back on the sofa and let out a breath. She took another sip of tea to hide her relief. "Of course. I wasn't worried. Anyone who loves Brenda's cooking as much as you do has to be okay." She gave a small laugh to show him she was fine. Of course, she was.

But could she trust him? A small niggle of doubt teased at the back of her thoughts. She once thought she had a good sense of judgement. Then everything had gone sideways.

"You can trust me, Bree. Tell me."

Bree felt a genuine smile this time. "Anyone ever tell you how bossy you are?"

Lucas laughed. "Just about everyone in my family. Stop dodging the question."

She continued sipping her drink to give herself time to sort out her thoughts. How much should she tell him? She decided to play it off as a trick of the mind. After all, that's what it must have been.

"I thought someone was following me. I got scared." She shrugged her shoulders and tried to laugh it off. She wasn't sure how believable it was. She wasn't ready to tell Lucas about Bryce.

He wouldn't believe her anyway. No one ever had. Everything was made to seem like it had been her fault, her fears, her issues, her delusions. Why would it change now?

*****

Lucas doubted Bree was telling him the whole story, but he didn't want to keep pushing her for answers. He did, however, plan to keep a closer eye on things. Her reaction seemed to stem from something much more than just being over tired.

He had seen real fear in her eyes when he had come up beside her on the sidewalk. He had enough sisters to recognize a secret being kept.

"Can you give me a description? I can keep a lookout while I'm on patrol, see if I run into anyone matching it."

Bree knew she didn't have much to go on, but maybe it would be enough to make him believe her. "He was too far away to get a good look. He kept his head down the whole time. Tall. Maybe a little shorter than you. A Yankees baseball cap and a navy-blue jacket. That's it. That's all I can tell you."

Lucas considered what she had shared. It wasn't much, but he would do what he said. He would keep an eye out for anyone who didn't seem to fit in, someone trying a little too hard to blend in. His gut told him there was more she wasn't telling him.

Lucas watched Bree stand and set her cup on the coffee table. "I need to get going…" Her voice trailed off as she realized she would have to walk home.

"Need a lift?" Lucas raised an eyebrow at her.

"That would be great, thanks." Bree smiled. Maybe the tea and company had helped her settle some.

"Just let me get my keys." Lucas smiled to himself. It seemed God might be helping him implement Plan B after all. He could stand being friends for a little while.

He would be keeping a closer eye on things over the next few weeks. He might have to swing into the café a little more often as well, just to be sure she was doing okay of course.

EIGHTEEN

Fiona huffed a piece of hair out of her eyes. She was working on getting more sea glass pieces made. Kate's wedding was happening as their busy season would be winding down, but they would have a slight rush for the holidays directly after it. It was hard to plan for Christmas when it was so hot out, but if they didn't work on the extra inventory now, they would be caught short later.

Fiona sighed. In reality it wasn't the necklace she was trying to create that was giving her difficulty, it was her love life. Or rather the lack of one.

She thought she would be married by now. She was pushing thirty. She once thought she would be happily married with the requisite two point five kids by the time she was twenty-five. It was now two years past that date, and she was no closer to wedded bliss.

Her mouth tightened. She never regretted giving up the opportunity to be married. She would have met her self-imposed deadline. In hindsight, she knew she had made the right choice all those years ago. Hank hadn't been right for her.

She just wished her biological clock knew it as well. She'd made peace with her decision after Hank left, but then Kate fell in love with Drew. It was hard sometimes to see her best friend enjoying the life Fee desperately craved.

Fee also knew she could be, well, a little *much* at times. An ex-boyfriend once told her that. To her face as he walked away from her. It stung at the time and over the years it festered a little. Maybe she should change. Try a different tactic instead of the "in-your-face" exuberance she brought with her everywhere.

She shook her head. No, she had tried that too. Briefly. Hank had thought her meek and mild. He had been surprised to learn about her true self. It was then she'd realized she needed to be honest not only with herself but with everyone else as well.

She had been over this time and again. She needed to be authentic. She couldn't be someone she wasn't and if she couldn't find a man who could accept that, so be it. But she just wanted a husband. She wanted a family. Seeing how happy Kate and Drew were together just made her want it more than ever.

Fiona's thoughts turned to Peter. She had first met Peter Grant over a year ago when Kate discovered he was her long-lost foster brother. Now Kate was marrying Peter's adopted brother, Drew.

This meant the four of them often spent time together. A lot of time. And over the past year Fiona began to develop feelings. Fine. She would be honest with herself. She had a crush on the man, a serious crush, but he was oblivious to her.

She was not a vain woman, but she knew she wasn't ugly. She was slightly above average in height for a woman at five foot eight inches. She had long, thick, wavy auburn hair and deep green eyes. And as a true red head, she had the porcelain complexion to go along with it. She had her Irish ancestors to thank. Needless to say, living in a beach community did have its occasional drawbacks but she had learned how not to burn, at least not often.

However, her looks seemed to be completely lost on the one person she wanted to notice them. Peter Grant.

She tried to push him out of her thoughts. She'd attempted multiple schemes over the last year to get him to notice her and nothing worked. Nothing. She was starting to wonder if there really was something wrong with her. Or him.

In a few months, she would be forced to be in closer proximity with him at the wedding of their two best friends. As the maid of honor and the best man they had overlapping duties. They would be walking out of the church together, into the reception together, and, oh gosh.

Her head snapped up as she realized, they would also have to dance at least one dance together. Wait. Are ministers allowed to dance? She didn't know but there would be music and dancing at the reception so she assumed he could.

A small smile crossed her face. She was going to count on the fact they would have at least one dance together. She could work with that. She wasn't beaten yet.

The smile grew as she went back to working on the jewelry she was creating. The store had a large stockpile of sea glass due to an early season storm last week. She had already made a handful of necklaces and earrings.

Her thoughts turned to how she would sweet talk Peter into more than one dance. She would laugh at just the right moment. She would be like Goldilocks and be "just right" the whole night. She began to hum under her breath as she worked not only on the jewelry but also on her plans to win Peter over.

A small bell sounded as the front door was pushed open. Fiona's head came up and in walked Peter Grant, looking slightly uncomfortable.

"Well, hello stranger. What brings you here?" Fee willed herself not to blush knowing where her thoughts had been focused for the last few minutes.

She thought of anything but how cute he looked today with his slightly windblown dark brown hair and his chocolate brown eyes. He looked especially handsome in his khaki carpenter style pants, running shoes, and a red t-shirt.

"Hi, Fiona, is Kate around? I have a couple questions for her about the ceremony." Not only would Peter be the best man, but he would also be performing the wedding ceremony.

"Sorry, you just missed her. She was heading over to Drew's if you wanted to try to catch them both together."

"Oh, um, okay. Thanks." Peter turned to leave but stopped suddenly. Fiona watched with curiosity as he just stood with his back to her.

"Anything else?" Fee knew what she wanted him to say. She wanted him to say something like, "Yes, I've just realized I can't live without you. Marry me." But she knew that wasn't going to happen.

Peter slowly swiveled to face her. Fee held her breath as she noticed with amusement there was a slight blush on his cheeks. He looked adorable. He also looked uncomfortable. Maybe he did want something more from her. She could only hope.

Fee watched as Peter started walking slowly back towards her. "Yeah, so, well, I just remembered something." He stopped again and scuffed the toe of his shoe.

Fiona just waited. She wasn't used to this unsure side of Peter. He always came across as relaxed and confident.

"You're making me nervous. Spit it out." Fiona couldn't fathom what had Peter so flustered. It was fun to see him a little discombobulated for a change.

"Well, as the maid of honor and the best man, we'll be spending quite a bit of time together during the ceremony. You know, making sure Drew and Kate are on track and well, doing all the things they should be doing and whatever."

Fiona stifled a laugh. "Well, I suppose that's true to some extent. We both have to say a toast. Have you figured yours out yet?"

"What? Oh, no, not yet, but I'm not too worried about that."

Fiona raised an eyebrow at him. "Then what?"

"Well, um, you see…" Peter's voice trailed off and his blush deepened. He scuffed his feet again. Fee tried to smother a smile.

135

"Peter, c'mon. Just tell me already. The suspense is killing me."

Peter took a deep breath and then shot out the words, "I can't dance."

Fiona blinked. "Come again?" She hadn't been expecting that. Not at all.

Peter sighed. "I can't dance. I don't know how. I never went to dances growing up. I hated them. It was nerve wracking to think I would have to approach some girl and ask her to dance with me. What if she said no? I never went. I've never danced. Not once."

Fiona bit back a laugh. "You have like a gazillion siblings, don't you? Drew can't be the first one to get married. Surely you've gone to other wedding receptions and danced."

"Never. Yes. No." Peter raked his fingers through his hair. Fiona was enjoying watching his growing discomfort.

He continued, "I've gone to their weddings, but I've never danced. I always came up with a good excuse. But I can't this time. This time

136

I'm the best man. I'll have to dance. With you. Help."

The look on his face shot to her heart. He looked like a little boy who had just lost his best buddy. She wondered how much this admission cost him.

She knew Peter didn't like to look vulnerable. He once voiced how he didn't think a pastor should ever look incompetent before the congregation. Something about setting an example.

It had the opposite effect on Fiona. It made her like him even more. She struggled to keep from laughing. It would seem she wouldn't have to do much scheming after all to spend more time with Peter.

"Can you be at my place at eight tonight? I can teach you how to dance, Peter. It's not hard."

"Don't you know? Kate and Drew want us to do a waltz as the first dance. I thought I could pull off the 'sway in a circle' thing, but there is no way I can pull off more. Can you help me learn the steps? I don't want to fall flat on my face in front of everyone."

"No, Kate hasn't mentioned that plan to me. Let me check with her and find out what song they're using. Meet me at my house at eight tonight and we'll get it figured out. I won't let you fall, Peter."

She gave him one of her megawatt smiles and hoped he saw beyond her words. She wanted this man to learn to trust her. Maybe this dance thing was what she needed all along to do just that.

"Thanks, Fiona, you really are the best." Peter gave her a smile and headed out the door looking less like he was going to throw up.

"Anytime!" Fiona watched him leave, her mind whirling. She grabbed her cell phone to call Kate to find out the details of the dance. Then she needed to get home and get ready. Peter was not just going to learn to dance if she had anything to say about it. He was going to learn to love her.

NINETEEN

Bree was enjoying a rare afternoon off. The cloudless blue sky was inspiring, so she had grabbed her camera to go exploring. Walking around the town for the last hour, snapping photos while trying to figure out what her next step would be, was helping to settle her thoughts.

She decided to head over towards the church. It was the longer way home, but she wasn't in a hurry to get back to her quiet apartment just yet. She felt a need for some peace in her life. She took in deep breaths and turned her face up to the sun. The sun felt good.

Between waitressing and working at the cottage, she was glad to have some downtime. She didn't mind hard work, but it was nice to have a free afternoon.

There was a mix-up with the paint Drew wanted for the cottage. He told Bree she could have a couple days off until he could get it straightened out. Then the café gave her an extra afternoon off for a "job well done" they said. She hoped it was true and they weren't trying out a new waitress while she was here enjoying the beach.

She still sometimes missed her life in the city. The life she had before Bryce entered it. She had friends she used to meet for coffee or just to hang out. That all changed though. Bryce made sure to sever all of Bree's other relationships, so she was solely dependent on him.

She hadn't really made any friends here in Haven yet. There was the other waitress, Ryann, who was about her age, but she seemed to be busy with her own family and activities.

The owners of the café, while lovely and motherly, were just that – old enough to be her mother. She yearned for someone close in age, another woman she could talk to and confide in. She didn't mind being alone, but friendship was something she really missed. It was one more thing Bryce had taken from her.

Bree sometimes missed the busyness of the city as well. There was something about being in a crowd of people you couldn't really achieve in Haven. That feeling of being part of something while also not. It was hard to explain to anyone who had never lived in a city.

She spotted the church ahead and sped up her pace. She was trying to push past her feeling of uneasiness when walking around by herself, but she wasn't going to ask for an escort everywhere. She was still spooked, but she was trying to be strong and confident. It wasn't as easy as it had once been.

She'd swung by the hardware store a few days ago to get a canister of pepper spray. She wasn't going to be unprepared again. It was tucked in her back pocket where she could grab it easily if she needed to.

She tentatively pulled at the front door of the church assuming it would be locked. To her surprise, it opened. That would never have happened in the city. She needed to stop comparing her current life to her former life. It was in the past. She needed to let it go and move on.

She stopped just before entering and turned to look over her shoulder. She glanced around but didn't see anyone. Shaking off the feeling of someone watching her, she slipped inside.

Bree stopped at the back of the church and exhaled. She was alone. No one else was in the sanctuary. She could hear nothing but her own breathing. Closing her eyes, she inhaled deeply and slowly let it out. She could feel the tension she hadn't even realized she was holding lessen slightly.

Opening her eyes, she took in her surroundings. She had been attending Sunday services here for a while now, but she had never been here like this. Alone. It felt different somehow. The energy that was here on Sunday mornings was missing.

She began moving slowly down the right-hand aisle as she looked at the stained-glass windows. She always sat on the left side of the church. She didn't think she had ever really looked at the windows on this side.

The first window included three panels. One showed Christ on the cross, the second showed a cave with a stone next to the entrance, and the third showed Christ floating in the air with his hands stretched out and smiling. She admired the craftsmanship of the windows. The details were exquisite. The images of Jesus were so well-made Bree found herself smiling in return at them.

"May I help you?"

Bree gasped and spun to find a man standing near the front of the church.

"I'm sorry. I didn't mean to startle you. Have we met yet? I'm Peter Grant, the pastor here."

Bree took a moment to catch her breath as Peter headed towards her. Her heart was racing, and she needed a minute before attempting to speak.

"I think I've seen you here before on Sunday morning."

Bree laughed. "Sorry I jumped like that. I thought I was here alone. I'm Sabrina Martin. You can call me Bree." She reached out to shake the hand he offered.

"It's nice to meet you, Bree. Anything I can do for you? Other than take a few years off your life?"

As Peter smiled in return, Bree realized he was about her age. She'd always thought ministers were older, like kindly grandfathers.

She realized how foolish that was. Ministers didn't magically enter their vocation when they were older. Some must start younger.

As Bree started to feel a slight blush forming at her foolish thoughts, she hastily took a step back and turned towards the window. "No, there's nothing I need. I just wanted a moment to think. I thought the church might be a good place for that. I'll just head out and let you get back to work." She started to hurry down the aisle towards the front doors.

"Wait! Stay. You won't disturb me or anyone else. The doors are left unlocked during the day for this very purpose. You can come sit as long as you'd like." Peter smiled as he gestured her to come back towards where he was still standing.

Bree stopped. She hadn't made many good decisions about her life lately, especially when it came to men. Could she trust him? But then, if she couldn't trust a pastor, who could she trust?

She shook off the thought. She needed to start making those changes she kept thinking about. She needed to get over this fear that was ruling her every move.

"Thanks. It's been a rough few months and I could really use some peace in my life." She started walking back toward where Peter was still standing.

"No problem. Enjoy. If you need anything, my office is just through that side door and down the hall. Just poke your head through and holler. I'll hear you."

"Thanks." Bree took a seat near the window she had been looking at and glanced up. "These windows are pretty spectacular."

Peter turned back. "They certainly are. Do you know the stories behind them?"

"A few of them." She pointed at the one she had been looking at earlier. "This one is pretty obvious. It shows the death of Christ on the cross, His burial, and then His resurrection."

"What about this one?" Peter pointed at the one next to it.

The window had a large tree on it. There was a man in a white tunic standing next to it, but the tree was towering over him. He had a hand reaching towards the top of the tree, but it fell far short of it, only reaching about halfway. The leaves were green and showed a small flock of birds perched among the branches.

146

"No clue. I can't remember a story about a tree. Well, there was the one song about a wee little man."

Peter chuckled. "That was about Zacchaeus, which is another story."

"Then I have no idea. I'm not good with plants. Any growing thing that encounters me usually ends up dying quickly." Bree shrugged and grinned sheepishly at him as Peter laughed.

"It's a mustard tree."

Bree turned to look once more at the window. "I think I have a vague recollection of the story. Something about small and big or…" She trailed off and grinned again at Peter. "Maybe my recollection isn't as good as I thought."

He returned her smile. "Look at the bottom right of the window. What do you see there?"

Bree squinted to where Peter was pointing. "Should I see something?"

"Go take a look."

This was getting weird now, but Bree stood and walked to the window and stooped slightly to look closer at where Peter pointed.

"I still don't see anything."

Peter came to stand beside her. Bree tensed slightly before forcing herself to relax.

Peter reached over and touched a small part of the panel. "What do you see right here?"

Bree looked. "It looks like a small, raised bump. What does that have to do with the window?"

"That's a mustard seed, the actual size of a real seed. And the tree in the window is what that seed grows into."

Bree took a step back to take in the whole scene again. She was amazed at how such a small seed could grow into such a large tree. "That's pretty cool, but I still don't know why that story is in the Bible?"

"There is a short parable in the book of Matthew where Jesus mentions a mustard seed. It's only two verses in chapter thirteen. He talks about how the kingdom of heaven is like that small mustard seed."

Bree turned to look at Peter. "I'm not sure I see the significance. All plants, including large trees, grow from seeds. What's so special about this one?"

"Absolutely nothing. There is nothing special about a mustard seed except one thing. Jesus mentions it in His teaching, and the story has been preserved for us in the Bible."

"Okay." Bree was still trying to figure out why the window existed and what the importance of the story was. There must be a reason it was one of only eight windows in the church.

"Jesus was encouraging his disciples. Being a Christian isn't easy. There are days when it's downright difficult. But all it takes is one small act to grow and to change."

It couldn't be that easy, Bree thought to herself. *Change is harder than that.* She was living that very thing right now.

"That small seed," Peter pointed once more at the bump in the window, "turns into a tree that can be between nine and twenty feet tall. It grows so large Jesus tells us birds nest in it. It's a reminder to us. It's a reminder how nothing is impossible when God is with us."

Bree walked back to the pew and sank down. She had once been what many would consider a Christian. She'd done everything she could to follow Jesus and do what was right. She had even been baptized one summer when she was a preteen.

She still thought she was a pretty good person, but she couldn't remember the last time she'd opened her Bible to read. She didn't even know where her Bible was or if she had brought it with her on her flight north.

She used to read it faithfully. Then her life became busy. Soon it was easier not to make time in her schedule for a few minutes each day with God.

"Feel free to stay as long as you like," Peter said as he stood. "The doors are always open during the day. Stop by whenever you'd like."

"Thanks. It was nice to meet you Pastor Peter. I've been enjoying your sermons on Sunday."

"Well, thank you. I hope to see you again soon, Bree."

Bree turned back to look at the window. Was it possible to return to the faith of her childhood? To once more trust God with all things? Even the hard things and the things that didn't make sense? She didn't know. She was still so confused.

While she knew it was true how nothing was impossible with God, right now she didn't see how she could ever trust God again with her life.

TWENTY

Lucas yawned and stretched his arms overhead. Sitting in his cruiser all day was boring in sleepy Haven.

He hadn't slept well last night. His thoughts kept returning to Antonio. It was the anniversary of his death. Lucas was sure he would never forget that day. Ever. It was the worst day of his life. Not only had he lost his partner, but he had lost his fiancée as well.

He allowed his thoughts to drift back to three years ago. He had been working on facing the pain. He knew he needed to face it so he could heal.

He and Antonio were working their beat in downtown Miami. It was a hot summer day and they decided to take a break at the smoothie kiosk set up near the park.

While Lucas paid for their drinks, Antonio flirted with the pretty girl serving them. Then they heard gunshots. Lucas tossed the bills down and both men spun to get a bearing on what was happening.

They saw a man racing down the path toward them. A SUV was barreling down the walkway giving chase. A man was hanging out one of the passenger windows with a handgun taking shots as the runner zigged and zagged. People were jumping into the bushes to get out of the way.

Lucas and Antonio hadn't hesitated. Lucas remembered yelling at the smoothie girl to get down behind her kiosk. He quickly grabbed his radio mic and called in the situation while Antonio bolted towards the scene.

"Stop! Miami Police Officer! Stop where you are!" No one heeded their commands.

Antonio continued sprinting forward. Lucas took up a defensive position behind a large tree. He called to his partner to stop, to get back, but Antonio just continued to race forward. It was only then Lucas saw the small child transfixed by what was happening, standing in the middle of the path as the vehicle sped toward him.

Lucas couldn't fire. It wasn't safe to take a shot without endangering either Antonio, the child, or another innocent. He could only watch in horror, praying his partner's legs would get him there before the vehicle.

Everything played out in slow motion. Just as it seemed the child would be hit, another man dashed out from behind a tree, grabbed the child, and rolled safely out of the way.

Antonio was going too fast and was unable to stop himself from continuing. He slammed into the front of the speeding vehicle, his head hitting the pavement as he bounced off. He laid still, so still.

Lucas unloaded his magazine into the SUV at that point. He hit both the driver and the passenger. The truck veered off the path and crashed into a tree. The fleeing man never slowed down. Lucas didn't have the energy or attention to give chase. He flung himself on the ground beside Antonio and watched his partner take his last breath.

Lucas rubbed his eyes to help dispel the memories. His partner was gone. He always felt he should have done more to save Antonio. He should have bolted with him towards the danger instead of staying behind. He should have done something. He didn't know what, but something. The feeling persisted even now.

The investigation into the incident showed Lucas had done everything by the book. It hadn't made him feel any better. Nothing would change the fact that Antonio was gone and Lucas was not.

Lucas decided to forge ahead with the memories of what else had occurred on that day. Why stop now? He turned to the next painful moment in his life. The one that happened shortly after being able to leave the station and go home.

He wanted to go to his fiancée for comfort, so he headed to see Jillian. He thought he was going to a safe place to let the stress of the day go. He soon learned how wrong he was.

When he arrived unannounced at Jillian's apartment, he had a surprise of his own. He let himself in with his key and found his girlfriend in the arms of another man kissing him for all she was worth. Lucas just stood and stared, dumbfounded for a moment at what he was seeing. Then he spun on his heel and left. He didn't trust what he would have done if he stayed.

Jillian caught sight of him, he knew. But she only drew back slowly and gave him a look that conveyed she had no regard for him at all. He should have known better. She had been pulling away for months, but he was head over heels in love with her. He dismissed all his misgivings as nerves about their upcoming wedding.

He scrimped every penny he had to buy her a ring she would think worthy. She simply commented how he would need to get a larger one at some point. It was a good "starter ring" she said. He'd foolishly been elated with her response. He remembered thinking how everything would be okay now that they were engaged. It hadn't been. Not even close.

Coming back to the present, he shook his head. He needed some coffee and a pastry. He started his cruiser and put it in drive as he made his way towards the Three Cats.

It was Wednesday which meant cinnamon rolls. He smiled slightly at the thought. A big dose of sugar and caffeine might help him feel slightly better in the short term. He'd pay for it later with a longer workout.

He used to think his life in Miami was glamorous and exciting. If that was the case, life in Haven was dull and boring. But he found himself looking forward to going to the café for more than just a cinnamon roll.

He was hoping Bree was working. He could use a dose of her sass and smile today. Just the thought of it brought a larger grin to his face. *Yeah*, he thought to himself, *it's just what I need to get me out of this funk.*

The last day they painted together she had been full of sass and fire. He grinned at the memory.

Bree was working beside him. They both were in a groove. Lucas sprayed a section of the house and then Bree came behind him and cut in anything he missed. They were almost done before moving on to the trim.

He didn't know what got into him, but he watched her as she worked a few feet away. She'd put her earbuds in early today, a sure sign she didn't want to talk with him.

She was humming along to whatever song she was listening to, and Lucas just couldn't resist. He raised the trigger on the painting wand and gave it a quick squeeze in her direction. The paint hit her squarely in the back.

Bree jumped and spun as she tugged out one earbud. "What did you just do?" She squirmed in an attempt to see her back as Lucas stood with a grin as wide as the ocean on his face.

"Nothing. Why do you ask?"

"Lucas!" She gave him a stern look, still trying to peer over her shoulder to see what had landed on her back.

"I didn't do anything."

Bree turned to look at him and just as she opened her mouth, he pulled the trigger again. This time hitting her in the chest.

Her mouth fell open as she looked down at her shirt then back at him. Lucas dropped the paint gun and bent over as he laughed. That was his first mistake.

"Hey Lucas…" He looked up just in time to see Bree take two big steps forward and flick her paintbrush at him. The paintbrush she had just reloaded with paint. The paint splattered him across the face, arms, and chest.

"Now, you're in trouble." He took a step forward. Bree squealed and ran. Lucas gave chase. Around and around the house they ran before they both fell on the ground laughing and out of breath.

"You'll pay for that one, Martin. Just you wait," Lucas managed to squeeze out between breaths. "You know how paybacks can be. You'll never see me coming."

"You started it. You got exactly what you deserved." She huffed out laughter between gasps for air.

As Lucas parked his cruiser in front of the café, he realized he had another grin on his face remembering the incident. Bree looked young and carefree that day. Whatever problem hung over her like a cloud, had dissipated in their playing. He wanted to do that again. Make her smile and laugh like she didn't have a care in the world.

He continued smiling as he headed towards the café. It would seem his plan to become her friend just might be working after all.

TWENTY-ONE

Stifling a groan, Bree heard the cook ring the bell for her next order. Working two jobs was tiring her out, but the outside of the cottage was almost done. They would be working on the inside rooms next week. Soon she would have her car back and she couldn't wait.

She was nearing the end of the morning rush. She was looking forward to her break in ten minutes. Bree had plated a cinnamon roll for herself and tucked it out back wrapped in a napkin. Brenda was famous for her weekly cinnamon rolls.

Bree knew she should skip it. She really didn't need the empty calories. She was looking forward to it all the same, along with a nice hot cup of coffee. She smiled to herself.

They were getting low on rolls. She was glad she had snagged one. It wouldn't be Wednesday without a cinnamon roll during her morning break.

She looked up as the bell over the door jingled. Lucas walked in. *He sure fills out that uniform nicely*, she thought to herself and then blushed.

She blushed a little more when he sat at the counter in her section. She hoped it wouldn't be awkward since she had turned down his date offer and cried uncontrollably in his arms. Nope. This wouldn't be awkward at all.

She remembered their last day of painting. She couldn't recall when she'd had so much fun. Lucas had looked like a creature from Avatar with blue paint spattered all over him.

Bree took a moment to check on the rest of her customers before heading his way. It would hopefully give her time for her face to cool slightly from the blush at seeing him.

"Hi, Lucas. What can I get you?"

"You okay? You look a little flushed."

Bree took her order pad and fanned her face. "Just a little warm in here this morning. Thanks for noticing." She forced a laugh hoping he would buy her excuse only to feel her face flush a little more.

Bree watched as Lucas tried to hide his grin. So, he had noticed her blushing. She felt her cheeks start to warm again. *Hurry up and order so I can run away*, Bree thought to herself.

"Just a cup of black coffee and one of Brenda's cinnamon rolls. Thanks."

"Sure. I'll be right back." Bree hoped her heart would stop racing and her cheeks would cool before she headed back with his order.

As Bree approached the pastry case, she saw Ryann grabbing a cinnamon roll.

"Hey, Ryann, are there any more left?" Bree knew they had been getting low. It was why she had tucked one out back for herself.

"No, sorry, I just took the last two for my table over by the window."

"No problem. Thanks." Bree turned and headed to the coffee prep area to pour a cup of coffee for Lucas. She took it back over to him with a contrite look on her face.

"Don't tell me. That table beat me to the last cinnamon rolls."

"Yeah, sorry. Can I get you something else?" Even as she said it, Bree knew what she should do.

"Sure, I'll take…"

"Wait." Bree interrupted Lucas. "Hold that thought. I'll be right back." She turned and hurried to the kitchen. Taking the napkin off the top of the roll, she grabbed a knife to fix the frosting. She popped the plate into the microwave for twenty seconds, just the way she liked to eat hers, and then hurried back out to the front.

"Here you go."

Lucas looked down at the roll and then up at her. "Did you just whip that up out of thin air for me?"

Bree laughed, "No, I was saving it for my break, but you're the customer. You have it. I'll get something else."

She took her pen and wrote up Lucas's slip for him. "And you can pay Colleen when you're done. I'm going to go take that break now."

Lucas looked up. "Wait. I don't feel right about eating your roll. Here." He slid the plate towards her. "You have it."

"No way. I'm not calling down the wrath of the sisters on me for taking a pastry from a customer. I insist. You eat it. I'll grab a hand pie instead."

"Then join me." Lucas gave her his most winning smile.

"I'm not sure I can…" Bree's voice trailed off.

"Yes, yes, you can. Here." Bree spun to see Colleen holding a plate with a blueberry hand pie on it and a cup of coffee in the other. "Go, sit and eat."

Bree hoped her face would behave this time. She arched an eyebrow at Colleen as she took the plate and coffee from her. Colleen just

165

smiled sweetly back as she headed off to make the rounds for coffee refills.

Bree set down her plate and cup beside Lucas and then walked around the counter to sit next to him. This wasn't awkward at all. At least that was what she kept telling herself as she slipped on to the stool beside him.

She decided to be proactive about the situation. It would be worse if she just sat here eating and not saying anything. "What made you become a cop?" That seemed like a safe enough topic. Hopefully. She took a bite of the warm hand pie. While it wasn't her top choice of pastry, it was most assuredly worth the calories.

"I like order. And I'm a fan of justice as well. I'm pretty sure it all stems back to growing up in the family I did. Large, loud, and lots of foster kids."

"Did you like it? The large, loud, and lots of kids part?"

Bree was intrigued. She'd been an only child raised by her grandparents. There hadn't been any extended family since her mother was an only child as well. It had always just been the three of them. In fact, her granny used to say they were the three musketeers. A smile crossed her face at the memory.

She missed her grandparents. They both passed away, one after the other, shortly after she moved to Connecticut. Bree saw her mother briefly at the funeral but hadn't seen her since. She was still living her nomadic life with little thought to her daughter, as usual.

"For the most part, yeah. I always had someone to play with or to fight with for that matter." Lucas grinned as he remembered a few of the epic battles he'd had with his brothers over the years.

"What about you? Any siblings?" Lucas sank his teeth into another bite of cinnamon roll. He stopped feeling guilty about Bree giving up her roll to him on the second bite.

"No, it was just me and my grandparents growing up."

"Where was that? Here in Haven or somewhere else?"

"I grew up in Maine, but it was north of Bangor. More wilderness and less ocean. I've been living in Connecticut for the last few years. I used to work in New York City. But I wanted a change of pace. And here I am."

"That's quite the change. I moved here from Miami. I'm still trying to get used to winter."

Bree laughed. "Yeah, that can be hard. I'm really not looking forward to it myself."

She took another bite of her pie and they both chewed in companionable silence for a bit. Just as the silence began to stretch a little too far, Lucas spoke.

"How about we do this again, but some evening and with a full course meal?"

Bree took another bite of pie to give herself a moment to think. She liked Lucas. She had been watching him over the last few weeks and liked what she saw. He was kind to everyone. He had a ready laugh. He seemed, well, normal.

But she still wasn't sure she could trust her instincts just yet.

As she was getting ready to open her mouth to politely decline, she glanced up and caught Colleen and Brenda huddled just out of sight of Lucas. Brenda caught her eye and mouthed the words, "Say yes!" Colleen was nodding her head vigorously up and down.

Swallowing the last of the pie, she turned to Lucas. "Sure. Why not?"

TWENTY-TWO

Bree stared at her reflection in the mirror as she brushed her hair out. Why had she agreed to a date with Lucas? She had always walked on eggshells with Bryce, worried about ticking him off. She never knew what she might say or do or wear that would annoy him. And when annoyed, he was frightening.

Of course, she hadn't known that at first. She thought Bryce was as sweet as Lucas seemed to be. Bryce used to be kind when she was feeling vulnerable. At least that was what she'd once told herself. Now she knew better. Bryce only cared about himself and his public image.

Bree eyed herself once more. "You can do this. It's just a date. It doesn't have to be anything more. Get ahold of yourself!" She spoke the words out loud hoping they would make an impact on her anxiety. She could feel her heart racing. She hated feeling like this, so out of control. It wasn't until she'd been involved with Bryce this began happening to her. She used to be confident about her appearance. Now, she questioned everything.

A knock at the front door brought her around. He was here. Taking a deep breath, Bree headed to open it.

Bree took a quick moment to smooth the front of the navy sundress she was wearing. *Here goes nothing*, she thought as she reached out to pull the door open.

Lucas stood on the steps holding a small bouquet of gerbera daisies in one hand. He was dressed casually in a pair of khaki pants and a button-down shirt open at the collar.

"Come on in." She stepped back out of the way allowing Lucas to enter.

Lucas stared a moment too long. "Here," he thrust the flowers towards her, "I brought these for you."

"Thanks. Let me put them in some water." Bree took the flowers and turned towards the kitchen.

She pulled an oversized mason jar from the top of the fridge and filled it with water. She popped the flowers into the makeshift vase and set them in the middle of her small table.

"They look lovely." She looked up to find Lucas standing where she had left him inside the door staring at her.

What was wrong with him? she wondered to herself. Did she have lip gloss on her teeth? She reached up to check and then second guessed herself and put her hand back to her side.

"You look beautiful."

Bree felt a blush coming on. She used to feel confident in her clothing choices and how she wore her hair and makeup, but in the last few months her confidence had taken a beating. Bryce had successfully destroyed her self-esteem in such a short time.

Lucas asked, "Ready to go?"

Bree smiled shyly. She thought she could get used to the admiration of a man again. Maybe.

"Just let me grab my purse and a sweater." Bree hurried as fast as her high heeled sandals would allow to the kitchen counter where she grabbed her purse and phone. She snagged a light white sweater off the back of the couch on her return.

"May I?" Lucas reached for the sweater Bree was still holding. "It is a little chilly out there tonight. The sea breeze picked up."

"Oh, sure." Bree handed him the sweater and turned so he could help her into it. His hands rested briefly on her shoulders before he stepped back.

"Shall we?" He held out his arm. Bree reached out and grasped his elbow. Lucas tucked his arm close and put his opposite hand over hers. "I'm looking forward to tonight. I thought we'd head over to Ellsworth, if you don't mind the drive."

"Not at all." Bree smiled. She hoped she was conveying calm on the outside because she felt anything but relaxed on the inside. Ellsworth was a good thirty-minute drive away. What would they talk about? What would he expect? She stopped. She reminded herself this was just casual. There were no expectations. At least she didn't think there were. She risked a quick glance to the side.

As they headed down the stairs to the street, Bree glanced into the backyard of the house and saw Bert sitting in an Adirondack chair in front of a small fire pit.

"Hi, Bert! Have a good night!" She wanted to be sure he saw her. Just in case. She kept telling herself to stop being ridiculous. Lucas had proven himself worthy of her trust already. Maybe if she had been more careful with Bryce, she wouldn't have ended up in such a mess.

"Well, my goodness, if it isn't Officer Lucas. You take care of that little lady. She's pretty special, my goodness."

"I wouldn't dream of doing anything different, Bert. My mama would box my ears if I did. Have a good night."

They continued walking towards Lucas's truck with Bert's laughter ringing out. "My goodness, you were raised right then!"

*****

Lucas pulled open the door of his truck for Bree. He helped her in and made sure she was tucked inside before shutting the door. He'd cleaned it out as well as washed it earlier in the day. It was never super dirty. He didn't like riding around in a truck with bottles and cans rolling around or trash all over the floor. He wasn't a neat freak by any means, but he did like things tidy.

As he jogged around the front, he recalled getting caught by his brothers earlier. Drew had arrived home and Peter had shown up shortly after to discuss wedding details. They found him getting ready to wash the truck.

"What's the occasion?" Drew shot him a grin. "Does it involve a pretty waitress from a certain café?"

"No, um, maybe. I think I'll plead the fifth." Lucas continued filling up the bucket of soapy water. "It's really none of your business why I want to clean my truck. It was dirty. Enough said."

"Right," Peter shot back. "Because it's filthy. Come on. Your vehicle is never dirty, Lucas. What's up?"

"He's been making eyes at the new waitress in town." Drew grinned at his brother.

"I repeat. It's none of your business." Lucas grabbed the sponge and started soaping up his truck trying to ignore the verbal jabs of his brothers. Having older brothers could be annoying.

"Hey man, we're happy for you. You know that right?" Peter grabbed the long-handled washing brush and started scrubbing the bumpers.

"Yeah. I can't be the only happy one in the family. You know I'm getting married soon, right?" Drew found another sponge in the bucket and started to soap up the other side.

Lucas stood and looked at his brothers. "Thanks guys. And yeah, it's Bree."

He grabbed the hose to wash off the truck and decided it wouldn't hurt to give his brothers a reminder of who was in charge, at least at the moment. They all ended up soaked and laughing and Lucas forgot his anxiety about the date for a moment.

Now here he was, a few hours later, with Bree beside him heading towards Ellsworth for dinner. He had already called The Roost to make reservations. It was a pub in town with a casual ambience, but fantastic steak.

"You mentioned you didn't grow up in Haven. Where did you live then?" Lucas attempted to get the conversation started.

"My mom was like a modern-day hippie, I guess. She wanted to see as much of the world, well states, as she could. She moved around a lot. I grew up north of Bangor, in a little town called Monson. I lived with my grandparents while my mom was off exploring."

"That must have been tough, not having your mom around." Lucas couldn't imagine not having his parents close by when he was a child. They were a close-knit family. He talked to his parents every week and most of his siblings, those that didn't live nearby, a few times a month.

"It wasn't bad. At least I had my grandparents. They both died a couple years ago."

Bree needed the conversation to move on to a different topic before she started crying and ruined her makeup. "You mentioned Miami. Is that where you grew up?"

"Not Miami, but in Florida. My parents were foster parents there. I have six siblings, four of whom they adopted out of foster care. You've met Drew and Peter. Those are my two older brothers."

"How did you go from living in Florida to Maine? They are kind of extremes." Bree gave a slight laugh. "It must be hard to give up sun and sand for snow and ice."

Lucas laughed. "You'd think so, but Florida is so humid in the summer it can be downright miserable. It gets wicked hot." He stopped and shot her a glance. "Did I use that right?"

She looked at him. "Use what right?" She was confused.

"Wicked. Wicked hot. Is that right? I'm still trying to figure out Maine slang."

"Oh!" Bree laughed. She nodded. "Yes, yes you did."

Lucas continued, "We used to spend vacations in Haven in the summer when I was a teenager. I could never figure out how to use that word correctly. I've been practicing. Thanks for not making me feel like an idiot."

Bree cleared her throat and felt a slight blush forming. "You were telling me about growing up in Florida."

"Oh, right." Lucas felt her eyes watching him but hadn't wanted to look her way. He realized he liked her checking him out. How long had it been since he enjoyed being in the company of a pretty woman?

"Peter was the first to move to Haven. He became the pastor at Seaside Chapel."

"Pastor Peter! I finally met him the other day when I went to the church in the middle of the week. He seems pretty nice."

"Yeah, that's him. Drew followed and now here I am. The rest of our siblings are scattered along the eastern seaboard. Our youngest brother just graduated college. Manny is working in Florida, but I wouldn't be surprised if he moved further north soon. He's an engineer."

"It must be fun to have so many siblings. I've missed having a sister or a brother sometimes."

"I guess. I didn't really know any different. I'm only three years younger than Peter and we always had extra kids in the house. Some of them just ended up staying forever."

"You have three brothers and three sisters?"

"Yup. In order there is Peter, Drew, me, Claire, Miriam, Sally, and Manny. Drew, Claire, Sally, and Manny are all adopted. My parents are retired now. They travel around spending a few weeks at a time with everyone. They're still based in Florida, but they only spend a few weeks there each year. Usually, they are with whichever one of my sisters is currently having a baby. Then they'll be here in Haven for the wedding in a couple of months."

"How many grandchildren do your parents have?"

"Just three, well, almost four currently. They love being grandparents. My sister Miriam just married last year. I expect a pregnancy announcement any time from her. Drew is marrying this year so that just leaves Peter, Manny, and myself as the unmarried ones."

"You all sound like one big happy family."

"What about you, Bree? What brings you to Haven? Are you going to be here for a while?"

Bree swallowed. She couldn't tell him the whole truth, not yet anyway. "I was planning to head north, but my car picked Haven for me."

Lucas looked at her curiously. "Do tell."

"I hadn't planned to stay along the coast. I was planning to head towards the Bangor area and see what I could find for work. But I ended up here because my car decided to die in the middle of the parking lot at the Ritz Gas 'N Go.

"Haven seemed like a good spot. Especially when I was able to get the waitressing job at the Three Cats the day I arrived. And even found my apartment. Everything lined up for me to stay, so here I am."

Lucas didn't want to examine the warmth he felt spreading through him at those words. It sounded like she was here for more than a summer. He smiled broadly at her and then turned back to the road.

TWENTY-THREE

Fiona bustled about her apartment tossing some socks and a pair of sneakers into her bedroom. She slammed the door behind her. She hadn't been sure what to wear and it showed. Almost every item she owned was strewn across the bed. Her closet doors were open with blouses hanging off hangers, shoes scattered everywhere, and drawers open with shirts and pants hanging out. While never super tidy to begin with, her bedroom now looked like a hurricane had hit it.

She wanted to call Kate for some clothing advice, but she didn't want to tip her hand either. She had never confirmed her feelings for Peter. She wasn't going to start now. Not yet. She felt the need to guard this, whatever *this* was. She didn't want to screw it up.

Her personality was larger than life. Her family and friends always told her this. She was quick to get angry, but quick to forgive too. She burned as brightly as her red hair.

It had been a long time since she'd allowed herself to feel like this, eager and expectant about a relationship. Her thoughts tried to jump back in time, but she pushed them firmly down. Now, was not the time to think about Hank and how he'd broken her heart. It had taken her years to get past it and she wanted to leave that heartbreak where it belonged. In the past.

There was something about Peter that made her go more cautiously than she ever had before. Maybe it was the fact that he was a pastor. She wasn't sure how a relationship with someone who led a church would even work. She wasn't sure if she was worthy enough for him.

She was trying to still be true to herself, but she wanted to get this *right*. She wasn't sure what that even meant, but she just knew he was starting to mean a lot to her, this small-town pastor, who says he can't dance.

She heard a knock at the door and kicked a pair of boots into the hall closet and squeezed the door shut, praying the latch would hold it closed. He was here. She willed her nerves to calm and threw open the door with a bright smile on her face.

"Welcome to Fiona's Dance Studio. Come right in!" She let out a nervous laugh as she swept her arm for him to enter.

Peter stepped inside with a bashful look on his face. She wasn't used to seeing this side of him. The side that wasn't preaching a sermon, where his confidence shone through in what he said. Or the playful side that came out around Drew and Kate. This was the quiet, unsure side. She wanted to change that, to give him a confidence boost. And to get to know him better along the way.

"I talked to Kate. She sent me the video on YouTube they're using. It doesn't look hard. I think it's going to be fun."

"Is it easy as in someone with two left feet can do it, or easy as it is going to take me all of the next two months to learn it and then I might still fall flat on my face in front of everyone? Define easy." Peter looked up with a wry grin. "This is hopeless."

"It's not hopeless! We haven't even started yet. I have every confidence in you. Aside from that, I have every confidence in my ability to teach you. I didn't take dance classes for twelve years for nothing. Now, help me move some of this furniture out of the way."

Fiona pushed the armchair back further and then went to help Peter move the couch. It was at that moment she realized she hadn't cleaned under it. Shoot. What were they going to find?

"Ready?" Peter leaned down to get a grip and the two of them lifted it and moved it back a few feet to place it against the wall. Fiona looked back and was horrified at what she saw.

There were at least six random socks, a pair of pantyhose, which perplexed her as she couldn't even remember the last time she had worn pantyhose, far too many crumbled up candy wrappers, a few empty and partially full water bottles, and various other debris of her life. She could feel her face heating. Dratted pale complexion.

"Um, let me grab a broom. I'll be right back." Fee leaned down and grabbed the socks and pantyhose and as many candy wrappers as she could fit in her hands and hurried to the kitchen. She dumped everything in the trash. Grabbing the broom and dustpan, she turned to head back to the living room and almost slammed into Peter.

He'd followed her into the kitchen with his arms full of water bottles. "I'll just empty these in the sink. Do you recycle? Point me in the right direction."

"Oh, um, yeah. You can just leave them on the counter. I'll take care of them later. Thanks. And, well, sorry. I should have cleaned all that up before."

"Fiona, it's okay. I grew up in a house with nine people. This is nothing. Some of my

187

siblings are complete and total slobs. Well, they were when they were teenagers. I'm sure they're better now. Maybe."

"Thanks." She smiled at him and went back to the living room to finish cleaning. While she knew Peter was trying to make her feel better, she still felt like a slob. She just didn't spend hours a week cleaning. In fact, she couldn't remember the last time she had cleaned under the couch, if ever.

She swept up the mess and walked back into the kitchen to deposit the remains in the trash. She found Peter still there. He was looking at the photos and items she had hanging on her fridge.

She wasn't in the "clear fridge" camp either and there was a hodge-podge of items tacked all over the front and sides. There were old ticket stubs, receipts, phone numbers, and photographs held up by various magnets.

"Is this your family?" Peter pointed at a photo in the very center of the freezer near eye level. It showed a man and woman and two small children, a boy and girl. The little girl was in a short green sundress sporting two long, red braids and buck teeth. The boy was in a green cap, green shorts, and a black polo shirt. The man and woman were holding hands and standing behind the two children. They wore similar matching outfits.

"Yeah. That was taken quite a few years ago before a lot of orthodontic appointments. Thankfully." Fiona felt another flush coming on. She silently cursed her Irish heritage. Why hadn't her family hailed from the island of Sicily with an olive complexion that soaked up the sun? Instead she hailed from the northern reaches of the earth where pale skin reigned.

"I think you looked adorable."

Fiona's head snapped up and her eyes locked with Peter's. Had he just said "adorable?"

Peter cleared his throat. "Ready to try this dancing thing?"

He moved past her into the living room, and she followed slowly. A slow grin spread across her face. This was going to be fun. And Peter thought she was adorable. Well, at least as an awkward nine-year-old. Maybe he'd think the fully grown twenty-seven-year-old was also adorable.

TWENTY-FOUR

Bree grabbed the full pot of coffee from the warmer and headed out to make her rounds around the tables. The morning crowd was beginning to thin and those getting a later start were trickling into the café.

She covered a yawn with her hand as she headed to the corner booth. She had enjoyed her date with Lucas. Well, she had more than enjoyed it. She'd had the best time in longer than she could remember.

He appeared as genuine as he always seemed at the café or Drew's. He never made her feel uncomfortable. Their conversation continued to flow easily throughout the evening. They discussed their favorite movies, books, and things to do when they weren't working.

She even shared about her love of photography and how that was what drew her to the city in the first place.

She'd decided to explore the harbor later today to see if she could capture some more photos of the coast. High tide was late in the day. She wanted to try to catch some nice breakers against the rocky shore.

"Need a refill?" She held up the pot of coffee as she looked around the table. Lucas's brother Drew and a woman she assumed was his fiancée were sitting with Peter and another woman.

"Please!" The red headed woman said, holding out her cup eagerly. "I'm Fiona by the way. You're Sabrina, right? Well, of course you are, or at least that's what your nametag says. How are you liking Haven?"

Bree took a breath because she was pretty sure Fiona hadn't taken one at any point in any of those questions. "Call me Bree. I'm really liking it. I've never lived on the coast. It's gorgeous here."

"How wonderful!" Fiona exclaimed before taking a long sip of her steaming mug of coffee. "Ahhh, that hits the spot."

"I'm Kate. I don't think we've met yet either." Bree shook the hand Kate offered her.

"It's nice to meet you." Bree smiled as she reached to take Peter's mug. She handed it back and turned to the other side of the table to fill those mugs as well. "Let me know if I can get you anything else."

As Bree hurried off to the next patron who was waving a coffee mug at her, she heard Fiona say, "She seems nice. I can see why Lucas is smitten."

She felt her face go red and she was glad her back was to the table. Lucas was smitten? Smitten! Who even says that anymore? She shook it off and continued her rounds.

*****

"I never said smitten, Fiona." Peter took another swig of his coffee. "I just said he took her on a date Saturday night and seemed mighty happy about it. Drew and I found him

193

detailing his truck when we showed up there to talk about the wedding.

"Speaking of which," he turned to look across the table at his brother and future sister-in-law, "we need to finalize the plans. You're writing your own vows, correct?"

Peter would be pulling double duty at the wedding. He would be both best man and he had the privilege of performing the marriage ceremony. It would be the first time he'd ever married a sibling. He was looking forward to it.

Kate smiled at Drew. She couldn't wait to be married to this man. She never thought she'd ever trust anyone again, certainly not enough to connect her life to theirs, but now she was getting impatient and wished they had picked a date that was closer.

"That's the plan. Right, Drew?"

"Sure. Yeah. We can do that."

Kate gave him a fake frown. "I thought we'd agreed. Would you rather use something more traditional? I'm sure there's a book or something Peter can use if you'd rather not."

While Kate faked the frown, she genuinely hoped Drew would agree to writing their own vows. She was halfway through hers after all and having fun. Every time she worked on them, she fell more and more in love.

"I know how important this is to you, honey. I'm also sure you've already started yours. I'll work on mine and soon."

Drew turned to look at his brother. "Yes, we're writing our own vows," he said firmly.

Kate smiled and glanced over at her friend. Fee, however, was not looking at Kate. She was watching Peter with a dreamy smile on her face. *That's apparently still a thing*, she thought to herself.

Kate lightly kicked Fee under the table. Fiona jumped and shot an annoyed look at Kate. Kate raised an eyebrow at her as if to say, *Get your head in the game, girl*. She watched as Fiona flushed slightly and ducked her head.

"I'd like you two to start premarital counseling with me this week or next at the latest. We have about eight weeks before your wedding. I have six sessions I'd like to get in before then. Are you okay with me doing it? If not, I can call a friend over in Bar Harbor to see if he's available."

"I'm okay with Peter if you are Drew. I'll let you decide on this one." Kate smiled again as she took another sip of coffee.

Drew eyed his brother across the table. "I don't know. Premarital counseling from a bachelor who's my brother? That seems kind of sketchy to me."

"Well, my friend in Bar Harbor is single too but not related. I'm simply going to share with you what God says about the holy union of marriage, and you can go from there. This isn't a do as I do kind of thing, you know." Peter took a sip of his own coffee to hide the sting of his brother's comment.

He knew Drew was joking, but it hadn't been lost on him how he was still single. It made him realize how much he would love to find a wife. He felt himself glance at Fiona at the thought.

Fiona was staring over Kate's shoulder with her coffee cup in her hand. Peter turned back and saw that Drew hadn't missed the glance.

Drew raised an eyebrow at his brother and looked back and forth between Peter and Fiona and raised the other eyebrow. Peter shook his head and glanced down. "What will it be? Me or my friend?"

Peter wasn't interested in Fiona. Not like that anyway. He just needed her help with this dancing thing. That was it. She was a friend. Just a friend. He didn't have feelings for her. None at all.

Peter wasn't even sure where Fiona stood when it came to her faith. She was coming to church regularly, but that didn't mean she was following Christ. Maybe it was time to find out exactly where she stood before their relationship went any further.

He held himself still at the sudden thought. They didn't have a relationship. They were friends. That was it, but as her pastor, he really should have the conversation with her. It was the right thing to do.

Drew looked away from his brother, but not before a grin spread across his face. Oh, he was going to enjoy this. First Lucas was all bothered over Bree and now it appeared Peter was in a similar state over Fiona. Peter and Fee were as opposite as opposite could be. Oh yes, he was going to have fun with this all right.

"I'm good with Peter. It's a lot closer and we know him already." Drew squeezed Kate's hand. He was so in love with this woman he wished their wedding was today. He wasn't sure how he was going to make it another eight weeks until she was Mrs. Grant.

"Sure. When do we start?" She looked at Peter and waited for a response.

Except Peter was staring out the window oblivious to what she just said. She glanced at Drew. He put a finger to his lips and sat back. He wanted to see how long it would take Peter, and Fiona as well from the looks of it, to realize no one was talking.

Kate grinned and matched Drew's posture. The minutes slowly ticked by. The couple glanced at each other with smiles and worked hard to contain their snickers and giggles. The couple sitting across from them was totally engrossed in their own thoughts and the rest of the world had disappeared.

Peter stared out the window as his thoughts kept going back to marriage and his lack of any prospects. He had enjoyed his time at Fiona's the other night. They laughed together and had fun working out the steps for the dance. He felt awkward and out of sorts, but Fiona kept making it fun, so it hadn't bothered him. Amazingly. He'd even been reluctant to leave at the end of the night.

They had still been laughing about their last attempt. Peter went left when he should have gone right and the two ended up so twisted and off balance. They fell onto the couch and bounced to the floor.

"It's a good thing you're like a Bumble and bounce, Peter!"

Peter laughed at the reference to Rudolf. Clearly Fiona shared his love of the best Christmas cartoon. "At least I'm good for cushioning a fall onto your hard floor. I can't seem to dance, but at least I have that going for me." Peter smiled back at her.

As he stared into her eyes, he felt his smile fade along with hers. He unconsciously reached out and tucked a curl behind her ear letting his fingers slide down her cheek.

He suddenly realized what he was doing and where he was. He was the pastor of the church, alone in a single woman's home, and he had just touched her in a way some, like Agnes Johnson, would say was inappropriate. What was he doing? He needed to be upright in all he did, not allowing anyone to gossip about his actions. He couldn't lead the church effectively otherwise.

He straightened and cleared his throat. "Well, goodnight, Fiona. See you tomorrow." Turning, he practically ran to the door leaving Fiona with a dazed look on her face.

Now he sat beside her in the café, only a few days later, and kept wondering what would have happened if he had instead leaned in and kissed her like he wanted to. Would she have pulled away? Would she have slapped him?

He was pretty sure the latter would have happened. She was vivacious and full of life. He couldn't see her thinking of him as more than a friend. They were too different.

And yet, he kept thinking about how she looked that night and there was a small part of him that thought she might have welcomed it. It was that part that had him staring out the window right now. At the café. Shoot.

Peter turned and saw his brother and Kate sitting on the other side of the booth quietly sipping their coffees as they watched him and Fiona. He glanced next him to see Fiona with her head in her hands and a slight smile on her face staring off into space over Kate's shoulder, with no apparent clue as to what was happening around her.

Peter leaned over and nudged Fiona with his shoulder. "Huh? What?" Fee straightened and looked confusedly as Drew and Kate started laughing uncontrollably. She looked at Peter for help.

"Don't mind them. They've just lost their minds." Peter took a sip of his cooling brew and vowed to get Drew back for this somehow.

TWENTY-FIVE

The waves were crashing against the rocky coastline as Bree picked her way carefully towards the breakwater with her camera out. She was working to capture some of the beauty in the crashing waves, the sunlight reflecting off the water, and the vastness of the ocean. She stopped and took in deep breaths. Peace invaded her.

Her grandparents used to rent a beach cottage for a week or two every year until Bree had turned about ten years old. They stayed in various small coastal towns. Those days were some of her happiest memories, especially when her mother joined them.

Bree loved the sand and surf the best. Her mother would help her build sandcastles and play with her. Bree treasured those times. It made it sting just a little less when her mom left.

She remembered one time, when she was about ten years old. She'd sat crying on the porch as her mother drove off. Her grandfather sat beside her with a cracked sand dollar in his hand.

"It will be okay, sweetie. God is always with you, even when we feel broken. Just like this sand dollar." Her grandfather handed it to her to hold.

"Why doesn't she love me enough to stay, Gramps?"

"I wish I knew, kiddo."

They sat together while the tears streamed down Bree's face. She should have been used to the feeling by that point. Her mother never could stay long in one place.

"Break it open all the way." Her grandfather reached over to poke the sand dollar.

"What? Why?"

"Trust me."

Bree did as she was told. She gasped as she saw the small pieces of shell that looked like angels fall into her lap. "Gramps! There are angels in here!"

Her grandfather chuckled at her surprise. "There sure are. Let it be a reminder that there is always something good to be found in our brokenness, something beautiful. We need to trust the good Lord to help us find it."

Her grandfather had been a wise man. Bree had forgotten all about the sand dollar until she'd arrived in Haven. There were some in her apartment and at the café. She was hoping to find one on her beach walks soon.

Bree closed her eyes and lifted her face to the sun. A smile came easily to her face. She was sleeping better. It had been two months since she'd left the city. Bryce surely must have given up on her or never bothered to come looking, either way she was beginning to feel safe again.

She was trying her best to ignore the feeling niggling the back of her brain making her wonder if she would ever be safe. She kept pushing it aside.

She was safe. She had to be safe here. Here in Haven. Even the name said it. Haven. Safety.

"Is that a mermaid I see down on the rocks?"

Bree jumped as she opened her eyes and looked above her to the bluff. She felt herself wobble as she worked to keep her balance.

"Woah there. Careful!" Lucas laughed down at her.

"Not helpful. Why did you scare me like that anyway?" Bree finally managed to right herself completely. She looked up with her hand shading her eyes.

"I didn't mean to." Lucas laughed again as he started to make his way down the path. "I saw you disappear over the edge but just at that moment Mrs. Johnson flagged me down to complain about some guy who cut her off. Some 'flatlander' she said. What does that even mean?"

Bree reached for the hand he held out to help her across the last of the rocks. She laughed at the perplexed look on his face. "It means anyone not from Maine."

Lucas looked at her. "I swear, you Mainers have your own language. How do I change from being a flatlander to a Mainer?"

Bree smiled at him. "You can't. You are either born a Mainer or you are from away. No matter how long you've lived here. It's the rule."

Laughing, Lucas reached back to take her hand and pulled her up the last of the steep path to the parking lot. He didn't release her hand.

"Are you okay, Lucas?" Bree looked at him curiously. He had gone still and was just standing there staring at her. She wasn't sure if she should be pleased or worried.

"What? Oh, yeah." He stepped back and dropped her hand. "How about dinner again on Friday night?"

"I'd love to." Bree felt a flutter in her stomach. She was liking this man more and more. Even when he went still like that. Almost like he was studying her and trying to see deep inside her. "Ellsworth again?"

"How about my place? I'll cook."

"Really?" Bree looked at him with one eyebrow raised. "Are you planning to get take-out from the Three Cats?"

"Hey now, men can cook you know! Some of the best chefs are men. And I'm not half bad."

"Well, I guess we'll see come Friday night." She smiled as the two headed back across the parking lot.

She only saw Lucas in the café now that the painting job was done. She had been able to pay off what she owed on her car and was finally able to drive instead of biking places.

"What were you doing down by the water anyway?" Lucas started walking back towards where he had left his cruiser, Bree by his side.

"Oh, just taking some photos." Bree held up the camera. "I've been playing around with photography again."

"I'd love to see some photos you've taken sometime. Bring something Friday to show me." Lucas turned and gave her a wide smile. "I wish I had something creative in me like that."

"I'll see what I can do. And you are creative!" She pushed him slightly in the arm.

He exaggerated a stagger to the side and looked at her in surprise. "When? If you haven't noticed," he swept a hand down the front of his body, "I am a cop. This is not a creative endeavor."

"There might be some who disagree, but you also work with Drew. That's creative. It's not like you're following a set plan or anything. You design what you're building. That takes imagination. Then you take raw materials and make it. That's what creativity is all about, isn't it? Turning materials into something beautiful."

Lucas looked at her slightly stunned. "Huh. I never thought of it like that before, but I suppose you're right.

"Well, I'm not all that creative in the kitchen, but my mom made sure everyone who came through her doors could feed themselves should the need arise. Do you like mac and cheese?"

"From the blue box? Who doesn't?" Bree smiled at him waiting to see what he would say.

Lucas clutched his hands to his chest. "You wound me, woman! As if I would cook it from a box. My mother would have my head! Homemade all the way. Still interested?"

Bree laughed again. "Of course! What time should I be there?"

"How about six? I'm working for Drew on Friday at his place."

"I'll see you Friday at six, then."

As Lucas headed back to his cruiser and Bree turned to walk home, neither noticed the dark sedan with New York plates tucked against the back of the building in the shadows.

The man inside slid lower as he watched the two laughing together.

TWENTY-SIX

Photographs were strewn all over Bree's small table. She was trying to decide which ones to bring to show Lucas. She was feeling a little nervous about showing him her work.

She finally picked two of her favorites and tucked them into a manila envelope. She set it on the counter for later. She would grab it after work when she came home to get changed.

One photo showed the Haven lighthouse at dusk with its light on and while the sun was just dipping below the horizon. The sunset had been full of reds and yellows that evening with splashes of purples. It had been breathtaking.

The second photo was of waves crashing on the breakwater. She'd caught the spray as the wave had hit. The sun was glinting off the water like diamonds.

Bree slung her purse strap over her shoulder and tucked her pepper spray into her pocket. The day was too nice to drive to work. She decided to be brave and walk. She was working to not let fear rule her life anymore.

The Seaside Chapel was just up ahead. She was enjoying the sermons more and more lately. It seemed Peter always knew exactly what she needed to hear.

He'd recently preached about the parables of the lost, the lost sheep, the lost coin, and the lost son. Bree found it all fascinating. He showed how God pursues the ones that have left Him, how God yearns to have them back.

She was reminded of how she had once been a follower. How she had raised her hand during a prayer during Vacation Bible School one year and talked with one of the workers after. Bree had confessed her sins and pledged to live her life for Christ from that point forward.

She couldn't even remember the name of the person who had led her in the prayer. But she remembered her face. She'd had a kind, sweet face. She'd hugged Bree after and said, "Welcome to the family, dear!" Bree always wondered about that. She was beginning to understand.

The sermon had impacted her so deeply, she searched for her Bible in the books she had brought with her. The Bible was the one she'd received after being baptized as a young teen. She finally found it at the bottom of a box.

She'd begun reading it every day, diving in deep looking for answers. She sought peace. Peace that God was with her. That He was fighting for her.

Just this morning she had been reading in Isaiah and the words stopped her cold. *"Do not fear, for I have redeemed you; I have called you by name; you are Mine! When you pass through the waters, I will be with you; and through the rivers, they will not overflow you. When you walk through the fire, you will not be scorched, nor will the flame burn you."*

She was clinging to the promise because if anyone was going through the waters and fires

214

right now, it was her. The threat of Bryce coming for her still hung over her head. She was beginning to realize there was nothing she could do to fix it or perhaps even escape it. She was still scared, but she was working hard to cling to the promises she was reading in scripture.

Then there was Lucas. She could feel herself falling for him. She was so conflicted about it. Bree knew she still had some wounds from Bryce that needed to heal. She just wasn't sure how to go about it.

How could she fully trust Lucas when she was still having a hard time trusting herself? Bryce had done such a number on her.

Bree had finally seen Bryce for who he really was the day she left for good. It was late in the afternoon. Almost everyone else had left for the day. Bree was still there cleaning up a mess of paperwork that had been dumped on her desk thirty minutes before closing. She was once more being blamed for it even though she knew just that morning everything had been in perfect order. She was going to be there awhile.

She went into Bryce's office to ask him about an important piece of paperwork she couldn't seem to find. She knew it should be on her desk. It *had* been on her desk just ten minutes earlier, right before she'd taken a quick bathroom break. Now she couldn't find it. Anywhere.

Bryce wasn't in his office. As Bree turned to leave a folder on the edge of his desk caught her eye. The tab had the name "Martin" written on it. She couldn't recall any client with that name. Curiosity won out and she looked inside.

Right on top was the missing piece of paperwork. She quickly shuffled through the rest and saw other pieces of missing paperwork, photos of her entering her apartment, photos of her driving down the street. She was horrified.

It was then Bree realized she could no longer excuse Bryce's behavior. He was sabotaging her at work. She was holding the proof in her hands. He was following her, taking her picture. She needed to leave. She needed to escape.

And she had escaped. To Haven. To this small piece of heaven on earth, just like the sign said as you entered the town.

And she was now praying she could stay. She wanted to stay. She wanted to leave her past behind her, right where it belonged. She didn't want to face Bryce ever again.

*****

Bryce slouched down in his rental car and pulled the baseball cap lower over his eyes. He'd been waiting down the block from the café now for hours. It didn't seem like Sabrina was leaving anytime soon.

He'd found a room in the next town over. He didn't want to stay directly in Haven. The town was too small and the people too few to hide effectively.

He'd followed Sabrina and the new guy she was seeing to dinner the other night. He fumed the entire drive there and back. He almost lost them a couple times on the twisting roads.

He wasn't able to follow too closely. She had to be dating a cop. Bryce didn't expect the guy would notice. After all, how often does a small-town cop have to deal with anything more than a jaywalker or lost child. Bryce was sure this guy never dealt with someone as smart as he was. He wasn't worried about getting caught. He just didn't want to give himself away too early.

The game was barely getting started. He had more ideas on how to really mess with Sabrina. She was going to pay for ever leaving him. He was the one who decided when the game was finished and it wasn't finished. Not yet anyway.

Each day more things were added that Sabrina would have to pay for. Her actions were unacceptable. She had forgotten who's she was. She was his and would stay his until he said so. No one left him. He was the one who decided when things were done, and he had not done that yet. Not by a long shot.

TWENTY-SEVEN

"Good morning, or should I say afternoon? About time you got up, you lazy bum." Drew smiled at his brother. "Long night?"

"Too long." Lucas's chief had decided they needed to do a DWI checkpoint. It didn't make any sense to Lucas since the closest bar was thirty minutes away. Haven had been a dry town at one time and since the county had changed the ordinances, no one had ever seen fit to open a bar. Yet.

However, Searsport and Stockton Springs, the two neighboring towns, both had multiple bars. People often traveled through Haven to get to one or the other. And last night his chief thought they should see if they could catch anyone drinking and driving.

Lucas had been up until three in the morning working the roadblock with the full-time deputy. Of course, the chief was home sleeping. Lucas didn't bother to cover his mouth as he yawned.

He finally fell asleep around four-thirty only to be awakened at ten by his brother hammering on the roof. He hoped to sleep in. He gave up though knowing Drew was on a tight deadline to get the cottage renovations finished before the wedding. He reluctantly rose to face the day.

"Yeah. Zero arrests. Only about fifteen stops. Thankfully Chief decided to do this while it was still warm out. If we'd had to do it in January, I may have quit and gone back to Miami."

Lucas finished the last of his coffee. He was glad for the caffeine hitting his system. "What's the plan for the rest of the day? Need help?"

"Yeah. Just finishing up the patches to the roof. Then I thought we could start doing some demo work in here to get that expansion built. It shouldn't take long. I want to blow out this wall here, it isn't load bearing, to make the kitchen a little bigger. Up for it?"

"Sure, let me just get my boots on and I'll be right out."

The brothers were soon working companionably together. Drew had been right. The demo didn't take long. The wall came down quickly and then started working on getting ready to replace the floors.

The cottage's laminate floors were worn through in places. The plan was to rip up all the flooring and replace it with a floating floor that looked more like wood. While Drew would have liked to replace it all with wide plank pine boards, Kate insisted the floating tiles would look just as well and she wanted him to save the cost.

They almost had their first fight over the floor until Drew realized it was better to just let it go. The floor didn't matter as much as his relationship with Kate. Although, one day soon he would need to really discuss his income with her. He did well. He had no debt. He could certainly afford to put in real wood floors. He wasn't sure Kate understood this though. Drew planned to make sure she understood that, while they were far from rich, they would be able to live very comfortably.

"Hey, you're going to Kate's tonight, right?" Lucas used the pry bar to leverage a tough spot up where he was kneeling on the floor.

"Yeah, why?"

"Bree's coming over for dinner. Just wanted to know if I was cooking for two or four. You and Kate can join us if you'd like." As soon as Lucas said it, he was hoping Drew would decline. He selfishly wanted time alone with Bree.

"Bree, huh? What's the story there, bro?" Drew glanced over at his brother. He knew Lucas had been hurting when he moved to Haven last year. Losing his partner and his fiancée on the same day had thrown him for a loop. It had taken him time to recover his footing and Drew wasn't sure he had fully done so yet.

"What do you mean?" Lucas shot his brother a glance. He wasn't sure if he wanted to have this discussion, but maybe it would help to talk it out.

"Just want to make sure you know what you're doing. Just looking out for my little brother."

"You're only eight months older." Lucas had heard this argument almost since the day Drew arrived in their family all those years ago as a foster child. At the time, Lucas hadn't been thrilled to have another older brother. Peter and Lucas were only three years apart and they had been best buds. When Drew arrived, it threw the dynamic off for a while.

Then one day their father sat the three of them down and told them they needed to figure out how to be brothers and friends since they were stuck together for the rest of their lives. Drew wasn't leaving. They needed to find a way to make it work.

223

That very night their father started reading *The Three Musketeers* aloud to the family. It hadn't taken long for the three boys to catch on to what he was doing. Soon they decided that banding together was better than bickering or having hurt feelings about being left out.

"To be honest, I'm not sure I know what I'm doing. I just know that I'm starting to feel things about Bree I haven't felt since ... well, a while ago."

"Just go slow, bro."

"Thanks, man. I appreciate it. I don't know where this is going, but I know I'm enjoying getting to know her better. Bree is so different from, well, you know who."

"Care to elaborate?"

"Bree's just down to earth. She isn't playing mind games with me like, well..." Lucas waved his hand, dismissing the thought. "Bree's just different, but a good different."

Lucas concentrated on the floor while he thought again about that time in his life. He remembered feeling like things were too good to be true with Jillian. She was too, well, too perfect. He had a few rough edges from being a cop.

He was always a gentleman though. His father would have his hide, even as an adult, if he hadn't treated a woman well.

Lucas sat back on his heels and looked his brother in the eye. "This time I am fully following God's leading. Bree is genuine, Drew."

"It's about time you wised up and saw what was in front of you, man."

Lucas reached over to shove his brother good-naturedly. "Thanks for having my back, bro."

The brothers smiled at each other and then Drew said, "Race ya!" And the two were ripping up flooring as fast as they could go.

TWENTY-EIGHT

Lucas hurried to finish the pan of food and slide it into the oven to bake. He wanted everything to be perfect tonight. His mom would certainly be proud of him. He set the patio table with a tablecloth, real dishes, and even a vase of flowers in the center.

He looked up as he heard Bree pull into the driveway. He set a timer on his phone and slid it into his pocket as he hurried out to greet her.

He saw her smile as she stepped out of her car. Then her smile dimmed before brightening once more.

"Hey, what's wiping that smile off your face? Everything okay?" Lucas crossed the yard to where Bree still stood outside her car.

"Oh, no, I mean, yes. Um, yeah everything's okay. Really. Just had an odd thought as you were walking up."

"Should I be worried?"

"It's nothing." Bree waved her hand in dismissal. "When do I get to taste this homemade mac and cheese of yours?"

"I just put it in the oven. We have some time. Want to walk the beach with me?" He reached out to take Bree's hand as she nodded her ascent.

Lucas remembered how happy Bree looked when she caught sight of him coming down the porch. Then just as suddenly, her smile vanished. He knew there was something in her past she wasn't telling him. He wanted her to trust him completely and she didn't yet. Until then, he would do all he could to earn that trust.

Lucas was convinced Bree was different from Jillian in so many ways, but there was still a niggling voice that continued to taunt him.

What if that wasn't true? What if he found Bree cheating on him like Jillian?

As they started down the wooden steps to the beach, he realized how silly he was being. While they were hanging out together more, there was no understanding between them. Bree was free to see anyone she wanted.

And that thought stopped him. He didn't want her to see anyone else. He wanted her to only date him. Even the thought of her going out with anyone else had jealousy starting to roil through him. Maybe they needed to have a conversation about where they were headed. And soon.

No time like the present. "Are you going to tell me what wiped that smile off your face?" Lucas glanced over at Bree. She had her face turned away from him as she looked out towards the ocean and the horizon line.

Bree kept her face turned away. Lucas waited. He could see she was struggling with something. He didn't want to spook her. He could be patient.

She took a deep breath as they reached the bottom of the stairs. Before they could begin walking on the sand, she turned to look at him. "I used to date a guy before I moved to Haven. He wasn't very nice to me."

"Define 'not nice to me'." Lucas wasn't sure if he should put on his cop hat or his friend hat. He waited to see what else Bree would say.

"I used to work with him. He seemed nice enough. He said I caught his eye at the Christmas party. He started asking me out after that, but I kept refusing. At first. He kind of wore me down."

Lucas watched the emotions flooding over Bree's face. She wasn't good at hiding her thoughts. He waited for her to continue.

"Anyway, we started dating. Casually at first. At least I thought so. Then things started to get more exclusive. Bryce didn't like it when I went out with my friends after work. He wanted me to either be with him or at my apartment. I finally gave in because it was easier than arguing with him. And he treated me great when I did what he wanted."

Isolation. So many women Lucas interviewed over the years said similar things to him. "He didn't like my family, so we stopped visiting" or "he didn't like my friends, so I stopped seeing them."

Lucas glanced over at Bree. She was staring straight ahead. He started walking, tugging her gently along with him. Maybe if they kept moving, she would keep talking. He knew there was something more to why she was here in Haven. She had been so evasive.

"Did he hurt you, Bree?" Lucas wasn't sure he wanted to know the answer. If she said, yes, he would have to find this guy. Find him and make sure he understood he would never hurt another woman. Ever. Lucas would make sure of it.

"No, not the way you're thinking. And it doesn't matter now. I'm here. He's there. He doesn't know where I am and I'm starting my new life." She gave her head a firm shake and looked at him.

Friend hat it was then. For now. He would set aside his cop side for a little while and give her friendship, or more if she'd let him. His heart jolted slightly at the thought of more. He was enjoying getting to know Bree, more than he ever thought possible.

He smiled at her as she looked once more out over the ocean. "What's over there?" She pointed at the land mass just taking shape on the horizon.

"That's Piercehaven. It's one of the islands off the coast. Maybe we can take the ferry over for a visit sometime."

"I'd like that." She gave his hand a squeeze as they continued their stroll.

Lucas's mind began to whirl. He wanted to get more details, but he didn't want her to feel like he was interrogating her either. He wanted to make sure Bree was safe. He wanted to protect her.

He looked at her and their eyes met. She smiled at him as they continued strolling back towards the cottage. He realized at that moment he wanted her to see how some men were made to love a woman. And he was one of them.

TWENTY-NINE

Fiona fluttered about her apartment. Peter was coming over for another round of dance practice. Drew and Kate would be getting married in just a few weeks. They were planning it for mid-October when the leaves would be at their peak. The ceremony would be held at the local apple orchard with the reception in the old barn there.

Fiona knew the owner of the orchard. Richard Mosely had bought the place just last year and spent quite a bit of time renovating it. He had turned the barn on the property into a wedding venue. Fiona thought it a genius move. An orchard could only be productive for a few months out of the year. The barn gave him the ability to have more revenue for the place.

There was a knock at the door and Fee straightened. She had been picking up a pair of discarded socks. Why were there always socks laying around? She usually went barefoot. Tossing them quickly into her bedroom and slamming the door, she hurried towards the front door.

She opened it to find Peter standing there dressed casually in a pair of beat-up sneakers, well-worn jeans, and a flannel shirt open over a white t-shirt. Fiona tried not to notice how well the jeans fit him or how cute he looked in his casual clothing.

"Ready for round two? Do you think your toes will survive?" Peter smiled as he stepped across the threshold.

"Bring it on." Fiona laughed, happy to have him in her apartment again.

Fiona caught a look in Peter's eye when she turned that made her hesitate for just a moment. A fleeting glimpse of something that made her stomach clench. Could there be more? She shook her head slightly and smiled at him.

"What?" Peter looked quizzically at Fiona. "Do I have something on my face?" He reached up a hand to wipe his cheek.

"No, no. You're fine. Ready to give me a whirl again?" Fiona put on her "friend" face and went over to where her phone was docked to find the song.

She must have just read into Peter's expression something she wanted. That was it. There was nothing there. Oh, but she hoped she could change that.

She tapped on the song and placed her phone back on the docking station. "Let's do this!"

Fee hurried to stand beside Peter so they would be ready when the music started. She began to count out loud. "Remember, where we start, right?"

"Maybe?" Peter had a deer in the headlight look about him. Taking pity on him, Fiona went over and stopped the music.

"How about this," she began as she walked back to where he was standing. "Let's just run through it without the music first. You can do this, Peter. Have faith."

"Okay. Sure." Peter groaned, "How did I let Drew and Kate talk me into this? I feel so, well, so awkward. I'm a pastor after all. I have an image I need to uphold in the community."

Fiona didn't rush to answer. Peter started to fidget. Reaching out she grabbed his hand and tugged him gently towards the couch. "Come. Sit with me."

He followed meekly after her and they sank down, side by side on the edge facing each other with their knees almost touching. Fiona reluctantly released his hand and looked him in the eye.

"Take this for what it's worth. Maybe there's even some verse in the Bible, but it seems to me you may be putting too much stock in your image. Does it say anywhere in there pastors can't have fun? That they can't laugh or dance or celebrate?"

Fiona watched as Peter stared at his hands. He finally sighed and said, "No, in fact, in the book of Psalms we read about King David leaping and dancing and singing and celebrating. I guess if the chosen king of a nation does that without reservation, I can certainly help my brother celebrate marrying the love of his life."

Fiona smiled and reached out to touch his arm slightly before drawing her hand back into her lap. She wanted to hug him for the little breakthrough, but she also didn't want to spook him. She smiled and stood. She held out a hand to yank him up to a standing position.

"I think you should loosen up a bit. Sing and dance and laugh and make a fool of yourself from time to time. It will make you seem a bit more relatable to those around you."

Fiona laughed and Peter looked at her. "Glad to know I'm already doing that with you." He smiled back at her.

"I'll have you know that you've always scared me just a little. That was until I saw you trying to do these dance steps. I finally realized you really were human after all."

He laughed along with her. "Shall we try this thing again?" He raised one eyebrow at her, and she found that the most endearing thing she'd ever seen.

She realized just how close she was standing to him. Close enough that all she would have to do was lean forward slightly and she could touch his lips with hers. Her eyes fell on the target, and she felt herself swaying slightly forward.

Fiona stopped herself and her eyes shot up. She found Peter staring just as intently at her lips. His eyes met hers and held them for a long moment. He suddenly took a step back and cleared his throat. "Um, let's start the music before I turn into a pumpkin. It's getting late, isn't it?"

"What? Oh yeah, sure." Fiona hurried over to tap play on the song and reminded herself firmly how they were just friends. Nothing more. At least not right now. Soon though, all bets would be off. She wanted to be a whole lot more than friends for the long term.

She hurried back towards him and gave him a blazing smile as she stepped forward into his arms. "Ready? Five, six, seven, eight, and go!"

THIRTY

Lucas pulled into the café and put his cruiser in park. Wednesday. Cinnamon roll day. He rolled his shoulders. It had been a long morning already. He had been waylaid by Mrs. Johnson who demanded an update on the car that had almost hit her in the parking lot.

He tried explaining there was only so much he could do without more of a description. She had not been pleased. He felt relieved when another call came in. The woman was persistent.

A minor fender bender had called him to the local gas station. The Ritz Gas 'N Go was a staple of the Haven landscape. The two men who owned the place had already been out talking to both drivers, whom they knew of course.

He took all the information he needed for the accident reports. The men shook hands and already had scheduled appointments with the Ritz brothers to get their cars fixed later that week.

Now he was looking forward to a break and, hopefully, a chance to talk with Bree. He pulled the door open and entered the café. Inhaling deeply through his nose, he really hoped he hadn't missed out on the deliciousness he was smelling. He looked casually around to see if he could spot Bree.

He saw her in front of the bakery case and smiled, but it slowly faded as he saw her talking to Bert's grandson. He didn't know Sean was back in town. He had left to go to college, or so Lucas thought.

He only knew him from a few pickup basketball games he played when Lucas first arrived in Haven. Sean seemed like a good guy, but he didn't like the way he was chatting and laughing with Bree.

Lucas stood and considered what he should do. Sit and have his coffee break like normal, turn and leave, or go punch Sean in the nose. It was a tossup between the second and third choices.

For someone who had just come to his house the other night for dinner, Bree sure did look friendly with another guy. Almost too friendly.

"Hey there, I had a good time Friday night. Thank you for cooking for me. Your mother would be proud."

Lucas had been too focused on how he was going to pummel Sean to notice Bree was now standing in front of him. He didn't know what type of game she was playing, but he suddenly decided he didn't want to be a part of it. He wasn't going to get duped like last time.

"Yeah. Sure."

"Is everything okay?"

"What are you doing with Sean Hill?" He hadn't meant for the words to shoot out, but he couldn't seem to stop them.

"What?" Bree looked confused. "Nothing. We were just talking about the odd things we've both noticed about Bert's garage apartment."

Lucas stared at her. Was she telling him the truth? He wanted to believe her. He so wanted to believe her.

"Hey man! Good to see you!" He felt a hand clap him on the back. "I'm in town for the weekend. If you have time, meet me over in the park tomorrow for some b-ball."

Lucas turned to see Sean standing in front of him. "What are you doing back in town? I thought you left for school." He felt like he was interrogating the guy, but he couldn't help himself.

"I did. I came home to grab a few things I needed. I'm staying with my grandfather since this lady," he pointed a finger at Bree, "stole my apartment." He laughed.

"Hey now, your grandfather rented it to me fair and square. You'll have to deal with the sofa for the weekend, my goodness."

243

The two chuckled while Lucas stood by helplessly. They seemed pretty cozy for people who just met.

"Bring your brothers tomorrow. You'll need the backup. Good to see you, man." Sean headed out the door before Lucas could form a reply.

Lucas slid onto a stool. His mind was whirling. He thought he was moving towards something real with Bree, something stable. He thought he could trust her, but now he wasn't sure.

"You arrived in the nick of time this week." Bree walked towards him with a plated cinnamon roll in one hand and a coffee cup in the other. "Mr. Edwards arrived just before you and was eyeing this last roll but decided to get a muffin instead."

"Thanks." Lucas tried not to sound gruff but he failed. He kept his head down and took a sip of coffee.

"Rough morning?" Bree sat on the stool next to Lucas and tried to get a read on his face.

"Why was Sean here?" Lucas blurted it out before he could stop himself.

"I assume to get some food. He stopped to get a pastry and a coffee. When he found out who I was, he introduced himself. We started talking about his grandfather."

Lucas took a bite of his roll. It tasted like sawdust, but he needed a moment to gather his thoughts. Could he trust Bree? That's what it came down to. If he couldn't trust her, then there was no point in this relationship moving forward.

"Have you been seeing him?" Lucas couldn't stop the questions. He knew he sounded angry, but he couldn't seem to stop.

"What are you talking about? I'm seeing you or at least I thought I was. I *just* met Sean. As in twenty minutes ago."

He turned to look at her. She seemed sincere, but then again so had Jillian every time she told him she needed to work late or was going out with a girlfriend. And he now knew it had all been lies.

245

"Are we still on for tonight?" Bree hated the way she sounded. She thought she didn't need a man and here she was begging a man who was making it clearer by the minute he didn't want her.

"I'm not sure. I need to get back to work." Lucas stood, leaving his half-finished roll and coffee behind. He tossed down a few bills as he walked away. "I'll call you later."

*****

Bree watched Lucas stride from the café, wondering what she had done to cause such a brush-off. A part of her wanted to run after him, pleading with him to talk to her, to explain what it was she had done wrong.

Another part of her was angry. Angry for feeling this way again. She was tired of feeling like the men in her life manipulated or controlled her for their own advantage. If Lucas couldn't trust her, then there was no point in a relationship. She wasn't going to beg or plead. She was going to stand tall on her own feet.

But a small corner of her heart ached. She heard a still small voice say, *Forgive him*, but she pushed it away. *She* hadn't done anything wrong. Lucas would need to apologize and ask for her forgiveness. She wasn't going to play the same game she had with Bryce. Not a chance.

THIRTY-ONE

Peter looked around his office for inspiration. He was struggling to come up with a sermon topic for this week. Again. He could go with something seasonal. Fall was coming. Or he could go with something topical. There was no end to potential ideas there. Maybe he should do a series on relationships since he was currently doing premarital counseling with Drew and Kate.

He rubbed his eyes and held back a groan. He knew the real problem and it had nothing to do with his sermon prep. Although, if he didn't get started soon, he would pay for it on Sunday morning. He couldn't seem to focus. His mind kept going back to his last dance lesson with Fiona.

There was a moment at the end of their routine where he held her in his arms and dipped her backwards. He was having a hard time getting the balance of it all correct. He was afraid he was going to drop her, so he often stumbled. He felt like such a klutz.

"Peter, just relax. You can do this." Fiona stood and brushed off her pants after he once more stumbled and lost the final pose. "Just lock your arms and put your weight in your back leg and not your front. You're starting to give me a complex. Maybe I need to go on that diet after all before the wedding."

She raised one perfect looking eyebrow at him. He looked down shamefaced. "I'm going to talk to Drew. This is ridiculous. Maybe he can talk Kate out of this. We can just do the swaying in place like normal people."

She walked over to Peter and held his shoulders. "Look at me, Peter Grant. Wait, what's your middle name? This seems to be a middle name moment."

He mumbled a reply without thinking, "Michael."

"Right, you listen to me, Peter Michael Grant, and listen good."

His head snapped up at the use of his full name. It sounded good coming from Fiona. Nothing like when he used to get into trouble as a kid and his mom said it. He locked eyes with her.

"You just lack confidence. Fine. I have confidence enough for both of us. You *can* do this. You *will* do this. Got it?"

He almost saluted her, but she looked so serious and adorable. He didn't wanted to risk what would happen if he did. "Got it."

"Now, let's run it again."

This time he remembered all the tips Fiona had ever given him. As the song ended, he held her in a perfect dip. Her arm was flung backwards but her eyes were on his. They held the pose for a moment and then Peter found himself pulling her towards him and leaning towards her lips. He suddenly came to his senses, panicked, and stood too quickly. They stumbled around in a circle until they got their balance back.

Peter now sat at his desk, head bowed, praying quietly. "Why, Lord? Why are you tormenting me like this? Is it the thorn in my flesh I must bear, like Paul did? Can you give me something else? Anything else. Please?"

"You know what the first sign of losing it is? Talking to no one." Drew came striding into his brother's office with Kate trailing behind him. "You forgot again, didn't you?"

"What? No, of course not." Peter started to shuffle papers on his desk so it would look like he was busy. "And I wasn't talking to myself. I was praying. Especially since my brother was coming in. I need all the patience I can get to deal with you."

He smiled at Drew before turning to Kate. "Hi, there. You sure you want to marry this big lug?"

"Yeah, I'm sure." She came around the desk to give Peter a hug and then went to sit on the couch beside Drew. "He's growing on me all the time. I think I'll keep him."

Peter grabbed the book they were using for their premarital counseling and went to the armchair next to the couch. "Alright, let's get started. Drew, do you mind opening us in prayer?"

Peter used the time to calm himself. He pushed thoughts of Fiona firmly to the back of his mind and hoped they would stay there. He worked to focus on the couple in front of him. He didn't want to let either of them know what he was thinking about or, more importantly, *who* he was thinking about.

"Right, today we're talking about finances. Have you two decided how you are going to handle all of that once you're married?" Peter sat back and waited. His role was simply to act as a mediator as the two of them discussed all the things needed to make a relationship work. So far, he hadn't needed to do much refereeing, unlike other couples he'd counseled.

Peter fought to stay focused, but his thoughts continued to drift back towards Fee. What would she have done if he had finished the kiss? Would she have kissed him back? If he kissed her like he wanted, would she have responded? A smile played across his face, and he closed his eyes so he could picture it clearly in his mind.

Peter's eyes popped open as he realized the room was quiet. Too quiet. Shoot. He had forgotten where he was again. Drew and Kate were both staring at him with matching quizzical looks on their faces.

"Are we interrupting something there?" Drew gave his brother an amused grin.

"Not at all. Where were we?" Peter straightened and looked between Drew and Kate.

"Well, we," Drew pointed to himself and then to Kate, "were here talking about finances. I have no idea where you were, but it seemed like you were enjoying it."

Peter's face began to turn red. "Sorry," he mumbled. "Let's get back to it."

Peter shot a look at his brother that said he would not talk about what had just happened. No chance.

He also knew Drew would corner him soon and try to pry the information out of him. *Good luck with that, little brother,* he thought to himself as he watched the two talk out their plans for their future. *No chance I'm spilling the beans to you.*

THIRTY-TWO

The hammer slid as Lucas hit the nail harder than he intended. He jumped back and just missed hitting himself on the leg.

He missed Bree. He was avoiding the café. His thoughts and feelings were still such a jumbled mess. He needed to figure out what to do without getting distracted by her presence.

He sighed as he settled back to the rhythm of hammering the studs to finish the framing he was working on. Drew had decided at the last minute to add a small addition to the front of the cottage. The home didn't have a large entry area. Drew thought the small room could act as a coat closet and mudroom.

Lucas didn't care. He had taken a couple days off from his police job since he had plenty of vacation time accrued. He thought he had settled the entire thing with Jillian. He thought he was ready to move on. With Bree. And now this.

He sighed heavily as he walked outside to cut the next board. Drew had run out for supplies and Lucas was glad for the time alone. He had been dodging his brother's questions all morning. He wasn't ready to discuss it. Not yet anyway.

Lucas pulled his safety glasses down and reached for the handle of the chop saw. He stopped as he heard a vehicle pulling into the driveway. He looked up to see Drew's truck parking and Peter's subcompact car right behind.

Great, he thought to himself, *an intervention. That's just what I need.* Apparently the "supplies" Drew needed were reinforcements to tackle his brother's issues. Lucas wished he had gone for a walk or a drive or anything other than staying to help his ungrateful brother.

He scowled at the two as they approached him. Both had looks of concern. Lucas growled under this breath.

"Extra hammers are in the toolbox. Make yourself useful." Lucas grabbed the handle on the saw wishing he had more than one board to cut. The noise would be effective at drowning out conversation.

He finished far too quickly and grabbed the two by four and headed back inside to install it. His brothers trailing behind him.

Lucas wasn't sure how much longer he could ignore them. He knew one of them, probably Peter, would start talking soon. He wasn't ready to discuss it. Not yet.

His stomach churned at the thought of watching it all happen again. Going through Jillian's betrayal had been so hard. He couldn't go through it again. He just couldn't.

"Lucas. Stop. We want to talk to you."

Yup, just like he predicted. It was Peter who started talking. He had his "concerned pastor" voice going as well.

"There's nothing to talk about." Lucas turned and started hammering the stud in place.

A hand gripped his shoulder. This time it was Drew.

"Hey man, we just want to help. You know that right?"

"You can't help. There's nothing to help." Lucas continued hammering the board. He brushed past his brothers to grab more nails.

Peter stepped up beside his brother. "Could you have been reading more into the interaction between Bree and Sean than was really there based on what happened in your past?"

Lucas glared at his brother. He hadn't told either of them about Bree or Sean. It was a small town though. Someone obviously had. Lucas didn't need advice. He needed to be left alone.

"Hey, neither of us know what really happened. Tell us. Maybe you just need a different perspective." Peter gave an encouraging grin.

"Look. I'm done. I thought I could trust Bree. I was ready to trust Bree. Bree, however, isn't trustworthy. Like all women, she took the first opportunity she had to betray me. I'm not going through it again. I'm not."

Drew took his turn. "C'mon, man. What happened that has you ready to throw in the towel?"

Lucas didn't like his brothers tag teaming him. Not one bit.

"Fine. If it will get you off my backs. I stopped at the café for a break. She was all chummy with Sean Hill. Laughing like they had known each other for years. It was obvious there was something going on, but she denied it." Lucas wanted to throw something, hit something, *do* something to make the ache inside go away.

Peter asked, "What did Bree say about it?"

"She said she'd just met Sean. He was in town to visit his grandfather and came into the café. He knew who she was because Bert told him about her."

It was Drew's turn to ask a question. "What makes you think she's lying about it?"

"I thought you'd be on my side. You're my brothers. That's what family does." Lucas couldn't believe that Drew and Peter were defending Bree's actions.

Drew tugged his brother around to face him, placing both hands on Lucas's shoulders. "Look at me."

Lucas reluctantly lifted his head to look his brother in the eye. He resigned himself to letting them say their piece, but it wasn't going to change his mind. He was done.

"We are on your side. That's why we're here talking with you now." Drew squeezed Lucas's shoulders and stepped back.

Peter stepped forward and took the hammer gently from his brother's hand and set it aside. He saw the anger building and wanted to remove the temptation to throw it.

"We're here to help you see reason, bro." Drew walked over to the counter and grabbed a water bottle. He tossed it to Lucas who caught it automatically. He watched as Peter snagged one out of the air as well.

"Okay, just hear me out. I'm going to put on my pastor hat for a minute and I want you to listen. Really listen. Promise me?" Peter raised one eyebrow at him.

"Fine. Whatever. Go ahead." Lucas would listen but he didn't think either Peter or Drew would change his mind. He took a sip of the water and leaned up against the half-finished wall.

"I'm going to be blunt." Peter stepped forward so he was standing directly in front of Lucas, forcing him to look at him. "You're projecting all of your insecurities on Bree. If you trust the woman, then you trust her in all situations. She told you what happened between her and Sean. Do you believe it or not? If you don't, why not? When has she ever given you a reason to doubt her?"

261

Lucas glared at his brother. His mind whirred as he thought back over the last few months. He started to examine his relationship with Bree. Did he trust her?

"If you can't trust her, then you need to be a man and tell her. Let her go. Don't punish her with your absence or your silence. Either apologize and move forward or tell her why you can't." Peter stopped talking as he saw his words hitting home.

Lucas wanted to trust Bree. She had been honest with him, even trusting him with why she had come to Maine. Could he say the same for himself?

Lucas let his head fall forward. He heaved a sigh. "I just can't do it again," he said almost in a whisper.

"Relationships are hard. Life is hard. You have to pick your hard. Right now, you need to figure out if she's worth it. Is she worth all the struggle or not?"

Lord, help me. Give me your strength. I want to trust her, I do, but I'm afraid to be hurt again. Lucas continued to pray. He felt his brothers each place a hand on his shoulders.

Peter began to pray aloud for his brother, "Lord, help Lucas let go of the pain of his past. Let him see the good You have for him now. Lead him in the way he should go. Help him to trust in You fully and completely to do the best for him, as only You can."

Lucas's mind raced. It was true. He was holding on to the pain of his past like a talisman. He needed to finally let it go.

Lucas looked up at Peter and Drew. "Thanks, guys. Thanks for doing the hard thing and knocking sense into me."

He started walking towards the door. "Don't wait up." He started running when he hit the front lawn and jumped into his truck.

"Where are you going?" Drew called after him.

"To apologize to the pretty waitress!" Lucas started the truck and headed down the driveway.

Peter and Drew exchanged a look. "Nicely done, brother," Drew said. "Now, when are you going to take your own advice?"

Peter shot a glance at his brother. "It's different and you know it."

"Is it though?" Drew smiled as he watched the thoughts race across Peter's face. His smile broadened as he saw something change in Peter's expression. Maybe things would be changing sooner rather than later.

THIRTY-THREE

Lucas pulled up outside Bree's apartment and parked his truck. He shut it off and sat for a moment, gathering his thoughts. He used the drive over, short as it was, to figure out what he should say. He wanted to make things right. He needed to make things right.

He knew how Bree's ex-boyfriend had treated her. He didn't want to be lumped into the same category as that. He wanted to prove men could treat women well.

He shuddered to think what his parents would say about it all. He knew they had taught him better.

Well, sitting here wasn't going to get it done. Just as he stepped out of his truck, he looked up to see Bree walking out of her apartment dressed for work. She froze as their eyes locked.

He could see the same pain he had been feeling reflected in her eyes. He stepped onto the curb and waited as she began to walk down the stairs toward him.

"Hi." Lucas swallowed, praying the right words would come.

"Hi." Bree said nothing else, just looked over his shoulder, refusing to meet his eye.

Lucas knew the ball was squarely in his corner. He cleared his throat and started. "I'm sorry. I blew it the other day. I overreacted to you and Sean. I was a complete idiot. Seeing you with him brought up some things from my past, things I thought I was over.

"You deserve better. You deserve someone who treats you well, all the time, not just when things are good. I wasn't trying to be manipulative. I wasn't trying to make you be someone you weren't. It was all my own insecurities coming to light."

Lucas took a deep breath before he continued. "I'm working on all of that and God is helping me through it. I'm so sorry, Bree. Can you forgive me?"

He held his breath as he waited to see what effect his words would have. He had planned out more to say on the ride, but once he saw Bree in front of him, he couldn't remember the words.

Bree finally met his eyes. Lucas waited, praying silently to himself. *Please, Lord. Please let her forgive me. I promise I'll do better if you'll help her give me a second chance. I can love her like I should.* Lucas paused. That was it, wasn't it.

He loved her. That was why he was here now, willing to fight for this relationship. Sometime over the last few weeks he had fallen for this girl. Hard. Now he could only wait and pray to see if she would forgive him.

"I've never had anyone apologize to me like that before."

Lucas waited. He didn't want to assume she had forgiven him.

Bree smiled. "I forgive you."

Lucas stepped forward and pulled her towards him in a hug. He rested his chin on the top of her head. She fit into his arms perfectly. He felt the tension leave his body as his hold tightened. "Thank you, Lord," he whispered.

Bree pulled back to look up at him. "Did you just pray?"

"I've been praying the whole drive over here. The Lord answered my prayer. I had to thank Him." He smiled down at her.

He felt his smile slip as he stared into her eyes. He thought he could lose himself in them. He was okay with that.

"I'm glad you're in my life. I'll make it up to you, I promise." Lucas took a chance and leaned towards her for a kiss.

"Well, my goodness, Lucas! It's sure is good to see you, my goodness. Am I interrupting something?"

Lucas sighed, "Hold that thought." He smiled at Bree as he stepped back. The old man had uncanny timing.

"How's it going there, Bert? Everything okay?"

"Mighty fine! My goodness, mighty fine. You have a good day now." Bert winked at Lucas before he turned to head into his back yard.

Old coot did that on purpose, Lucas thought. Turning back to Bree he asked, "Need a lift? I'm dying for some pastries from the café."

Bree laughed. "I have some errands to run after work. Follow me there and I'll make sure you get whatever is fresh out of the oven."

"It's a deal." Lucas stepped forward and ran a thumb down her cheek. "Can I see you tonight then?"

"I'd like that. I'd like that a lot."

Lucas whistled as he walked to his truck and got in. Today had turned out to be a good day after all. He started his truck and waited for Bree before easing out to follow behind her to the café.

Both were so caught up in their own thoughts, that neither noticed the black sedan

269

parked further down the block. It joined their small parade heading to the café.

THIRTY-FOUR

Mornings had the nip of fall to them now that September was here. While some days were still warm. Maine in the fall never could make up its mind about the weather.

Bree smiled to herself. She couldn't believe Lucas had apologized. She'd all but given up on the relationship after three days of not hearing from him. She'd been working through her emotions when he suddenly showed up as she was heading to work.

When he began to apologize, she had started to feel like it had been when Bryce used to do the same thing. But Lucas didn't treat her like Bryce had. He wasn't trying to cut her off from other people. He wasn't controlling. He was honest and contrite.

271

She reached into the back of her car to snag the items she'd picked up from the store after work. She juggled her keys in one hand as she struggled not to drop anything. She finally managed to slip the correct key in the lock and open the door.

Lucas followed her to work and then sat at the counter for over an hour chatting with her between customers. He was coming over for dinner tonight. She didn't have much time to get it started if she wanted to grab a shower as well. She didn't want to smell like the café.

Bree's foot hit something slippery, and she bobbled for a moment before getting her balance. She looked down and saw a white envelope with just her name written on the front.

How did that get there? She stopped to pick it up with one hand and continued to walk towards the kitchen island to drop her packages and keys. Normally Bert just called out to her if he wanted to tell her something. He'd never put anything through the mail slot before. He never called her Sabrina either, but it was written boldly in block letters on the front.

The envelope was unsealed with the flap tucked into the back. She pulled the flap free and found a single piece of white cardstock inside. It simply said, "You can't hide" in large block letters.

The card slipped from Bree's numb fingers and fluttered to the floor as she swayed. Grabbing the counter, she held on with both hands. Bryce had found her. How had he found her? Her vision began to darken around the edges. She pulled herself together and whirled towards the door. She stumbled towards it and bolted it.

She turned to look frantically around the apartment. Was he here? Should she leave? But it was getting dark outside. What if he'd followed her and was outside now waiting for her to leave?

Was Bert home? Was he safe? She didn't know. She couldn't remember if his car was in the garage when she parked or not.

She fought off the rising panic and patted her pockets looking for her cell phone. Lucas. She needed Lucas.

She tried to control her shaking as she made her way back to the island. Her phone was not in her back pocket where she usually slid it for safekeeping. It must have been in her hand when she came in. She spied it sitting on the counter next to her keys.

Grabbing it, she pulled up Lucas's contact as quickly as her trembling hands would allow. *Hurry! Hurry!* It was all she could think as she waited for him to pick up.

"Hey there. What's up? I'm almost home. I was going to change first. Do you need me to pick up anything?"

Bree took a shaking breath. "I need you. Now. Hurry."

While Lucas loved the words, they weren't said with the tone he dreamed about. Instantly, his instincts were on high alert. "What's wrong?" Lucas had been slowing down to make the turn into Drew's house, but now he pulled a U-turn and sped up as he headed back to town. "Where are you?"

"My place. Hurry. Please." Bree started to shake at the sound of Lucas's voice.

"Is anyone there? Talk to me." Bree's apartment was on the edge of town. Normally it took him only five minutes or less to get there. Today it seemed like his truck had a large parachute on the back slowing him down.

"No. Yes. I don't know. Just hurry."

"Lock yourself in the bathroom. Now. I'm not hanging up. I'll be there in two minutes."

Lucas pushed the accelerator faster and wished he were in his cruiser, so he could use his lights and siren. But that might scare away whoever was there, and Lucas wanted nothing more than to catch the person responsible for scaring Bree. He wanted to put an end to the terror he heard in her voice.

275

He saw the mouth of her driveway and slowed down only as much as he needed to, so he didn't end up in the ditch. He felt his back tires slide all the same and dropped the phone on the seat beside him to use both hands to steer. He slammed on the brakes as he came into the yard.

He threw the truck into park and grabbed his off-duty pistol from his ankle holster. He jumped out and ran up the stairs to her apartment. He tried to open the kitchen door, but it was locked. *Good girl*, he thought as he pounded on it.

"My goodness, what's going on up there? Everything okay?"

Lucas looked down and saw Bert at the bottom of the stairs. "Go back inside, Bert. I'll be down in a minute to explain. Lock the door behind you."

He watched as the old man hurried inside and did as he was told. Lucas turned back to the door and banged again.

"Bree! It's me! If you're okay, let me in. Otherwise, I am kicking this door down in five seconds."

He began to count loudly as he tried to control the adrenaline running through him. He knew how long five seconds could feel. Right now, it felt like ten minutes. Just as he was raising his foot to start working on the door, he heard a click.

Bree yanked open the door and ran into his arms sobbing. He thumbed the safety on and tucked the gun into the back of his jeans as he grabbed her with one arm tightly.

"Shhhh…it's okay. It's going to be okay. Tell me what happened." Lucas ran a hand down the back of her head as she shook in his arms. He held her tightly.

"There…there was a note. On the floor. I just found it. It's him, Lucas. I don't know how he found me, but he did."

Lucas gently pulled her arms down and looked her in the eye. "I think it's time you told me everything. But first I am going to clear the

277

apartment. Follow me and stay directly behind me. Got it?"

Bree nodded. Her eyes widened as she saw Lucas draw the gun from his waistband.

"Hang onto my belt. And stay *right* behind me."

Lucas felt Bree's hands take hold and he began moving slowly around the cottage looking for whoever had scared Bree this badly. He didn't really want to take her along because if he did find someone it could get ugly fast, but he also didn't want to leave her alone either.

He made quick work of the tiny apartment and led her back to the kitchen by one hand. "Come with me." He pulled her behind him down the stairs and knocked on Bert's door.

Bert opened it quickly, a double-barreled shotgun in one arm. "My goodness, Lucas. I was just about to head upstairs to see if you needed any help."

"Thanks, Bert. No need. Anyone else inside with you?"

278

"My goodness, no, Lucas. I'm here all by myself, my goodness. What's going on?"

"Just had a little scare. Bree found a note under her door just now. You don't happen to know anything about it do you? See anyone come or go?"

"No, not at all. My goodness. Are you okay, Bree?"

Bree pulled herself together as much as she could. "I'm okay, Bert. Just a little shook up."

"Thanks, Bert. Lock the door though and don't let in any strangers." Lucas gave him a grin and then tugged Bree back up the stairs to her place.

"Give me a minute." He helped Bree to the couch, wrapped a blanket he found lying on the back around her shoulders, and then walked into the kitchen.

He called Drew. Lucas tapped his foot as he waited for his brother to pick up.

Lucas looked over at Bree to see if she was doing okay. She very much was not doing okay. She sat with both arms wrapped around her middle, shaking slightly with tears streaming down her face.

"Hey, I thought you were coming home. What's up?"

"I'm at Bree's. There was an incident. I am going to be here for a bit." Lucas tried to ease the tension in his voice, but he still felt adrenaline pumping through his veins.

"What do you mean 'an incident'? Is she okay? Do you need help?"

"Yes, she's okay. No, I don't need help. She's had a scare. I can't go into details right now. I'm not sure if I'm bunking here on the couch tonight or if we might come back there. Just wanted to let you know what was going on. I'll fill you in later."

"I'll be praying, bro. Take care."

Lucas sat beside Bree and pulled her in close. He wanted to go find this guy. He hated how scared Bree looked. He wanted to fix it. But first he needed to make sure she was safe.

Bree worked to pull herself together. She looked at Lucas and felt herself begin to relax

slightly. "Thank you. Thank you for coming."
She tried to smile at him, but it fell short.

"Bree, look at me." Lucas gently reached for
her hand. "Tell me what's going on. All of it.
Now." His cop face was firmly in place this
time.

*****

"I mentioned to you how the guy I dated
before coming to Haven didn't want me
spending time with anyone else."

Lucas nodded slowly. "You said his name
was Bryce, right? I'm going to need his full
name so I can start looking for him."

He was working to keep all emotion off his
face. He knew if he let his emotions show right
now, she might shut down. And if he was going
to protect her, he needed to know everything.

"Yes, Bryce. Bryce Weyhouser. He started
stalking me. I didn't realize it at first, but then
weird things started to happen. My car would
be unlocked even though I never left it like
that. Things would be moved around in my
apartment. Little stuff. Like my toothbrush

would be on the counter instead of the holder or my hairbrush would be in a different drawer than I usually left it."

"Did you give him keys to your apartment and car?"

"No, but he must have had copies made without me knowing. He could have taken them from my purse at work one day and returned them before I missed them. I stopped leaving anything of value in my car and I had a new deadbolt installed on my front door."

"Was this before or after you broke it off?"

"After. But I was still working at the same place. Then he slowly started poisoning people against me. Again, just small things. 'Someone' messed with the coffee and somehow, I was blamed. Information packets were put together and then sent to the wrong clients. Again, I was blamed even though they weren't always my clients or accounts. There was no proof any of it was me. Just office rumor. Good office rumor and finger pointing. All of it came from him."

"What happened then?"

"I was working late one night, trying to clean up yet another mess I was told I made. I went into Bryce's office to see if he had a piece of paperwork I needed. He wasn't there, but there was a file with my last name on it. Inside it were documents, most of them the missing files, including the one I was trying to find."

Bree took a shuddering breath as she continued, "There were also photos of me taken from a distance when I was out. Surveillance type photos."

She felt Lucas tense beside her, but he kept quiet. She continued. It felt good to finally tell someone else, someone who might believe her. "My co-workers thought I was bitter about the breakup. He made sure no one knew I had broken up with him. He made it look as if he had left me because I was some crazy woman. Then he started setting it up to look like I was incompetent at work. And he was succeeding."

Bree took a shuddering breath. She thought she had left all of it behind her. Talking about it again was bringing it all back, including the fear, anger, and frustration.

Lucas stood and started pacing in front of her. He stopped and looked at her. "Right. You have a couple choices to make right now. We'll deal with the rest of it in the morning. I can either stay here with you tonight..."

Bree's eyes jumped to his face in shock. She hadn't thought Lucas would ever make that kind of offer and certainly not in a situation like this.

Lucas gave a wry smile. "...on the couch. Or you come to my place. You're not going to stay here alone with just Bert to protect you. Even with that shotgun of his. Not until we either catch this guy or we make sure he's gone.

"Either I stay here with you, or you come and stay with Drew and me. The question is my couch or yours?" He waggled his eyebrows a little to help lighten the mood. It had the intended effect as a smile briefly crossed Bree's face.

"Yours. I don't want to put Bert in danger. It's obvious Bryce must know where I live. He most likely knows Bert is the only other person around. I can't stay here now."

"Then go grab what you need while I do another check to make sure everything's secure. I'll text Drew to let him know."

Bree headed to her bedroom to grab a duffle bag and stuff some clothes and toiletries into it for her overnight stay. She could come back tomorrow to grab anything else she might need.

She didn't know what to do after tonight. She just knew that for now she'd be safe with Lucas.

THIRTY-FIVE

Bree rubbed her eyes. She hadn't been sleeping well on the couch at Lucas's the last few days. He had spent the weekend installing a security system in her apartment with an app for her phone. He might feel better about having it in place, but she wasn't comfortable with the thought of only Bert downstairs with a shotgun to protect her if Bryce showed up. She didn't really have a choice though.

It was out of the question for Lucas to stay with her and she couldn't continue sleeping on his couch either. The wedding was getting closer. Lucas would be moving to a new apartment. Bree was sure the newlyweds wouldn't want her sleeping on their couch.

Lucas was driving her to and from work each day. He was being protective, but she knew she needed to start living again on her own.

Or maybe it was time to run, but Bryce had found her once. He could certainly find her again. There was no guarantee he wouldn't follow her if she left Haven. And leaving Haven meant leaving Lucas. She wasn't sure what she should do.

She had been wrestling with the dilemma for days. She'd barely been able to hide what was going on from everyone at work. She thought about calling out sick, but that wouldn't have solved anything.

Just yesterday, Abigail cornered her in the freezer. "Everything okay? You seem a bit off lately."

"I'm fine. I just haven't slept well the last few nights. I'm a little tired is all." Bree didn't want to lie, and it was the truth. She hadn't slept well, but she didn't want to tell Abigail *why* she wasn't sleeping well.

"Maybe you need the afternoon off. I'm sure Ryann could cover. I can give her a call."

"That's okay. I'll be fine. Besides, my shift is almost over. By the time Ryann gets here, it'll be too late. Lucas will be in soon and he's going to run me home."

"Lucas, huh?" Abigail gave her a shrewd look. "Are things getting serious?"

"What? Serious? I don't know. Maybe." Bree played up the confusion. She dropped his name for this very reason. She hoped it was enough to get Abigail to stop asking questions. She didn't want to have to explain the mess that had followed her to Haven.

"I'd better go check on my tables." Bree slipped past and hurried back out front.

Now, here she was contemplating running again. There was no more indications Bryce was around. He n't been spotted yet. Lucas had told her none of the local cops had reported anything.

There was only the note, but she wasn't a fool. She knew he was still out there. She could feel it. It's why she wasn't sleeping. She didn't want to put anyone in danger because of her. She wasn't worth it.

Lucas. She felt like her heart stopped for a moment. She wanted to save him from Bryce's wrath, but she would miss him, so much. It was the first time in forever she felt safe and cared for. Tears welled in her eyes at the thought of leaving him behind, but she had no choice.

Bree knew she couldn't sit on the couch any longer wrestling with the decision. She brushed her tears away and stood. She needed to get ready for work.

She padded down the hall to the bathroom just as a door to her right opened. She jumped, startled to see Lucas standing there with a sleepy smile on his face. He was wearing a pair of lounge pants and no shirt. His hair was tousled. It was obvious he had just rolled out of bed. She gulped.

"Morning." She squeaked out feeling a hot flush coming over her. Figures. She was standing there clutching her clothes, oh gosh she hoped her underclothes weren't visible, blushing like a schoolgirl.

"Morning, beautiful. I'm going to go make some coffee. Want any?"

"Sure. I'm just going to grab a shower first." Bree scurried down the hall hoping Lucas hadn't noticed her blush.

*****

Lucas smiled to himself as he padded down the hall to the kitchen in his bare feet. Bree had been getting up before him since she started sleeping on the couch. He considered himself an early riser, but every morning so far, he rose to find her in the kitchen, fully dressed, and sipping coffee.

He'd set his alarm for an hour earlier today and it paid off. He wanted to see what she looked like after she tumbled out of bed. He wasn't disappointed. She was even more beautiful first thing in the morning.

The smile stayed on his face as he prepared coffee. He grabbed a carton of eggs from the fridge and decided to toss together omelets for them. He knew his brother was already gone.

Drew needed some supplies from Bangor, and he'd wanted to get there when the stores opened. That would give them time to finish up the last of the projects here at the cottage.

The wedding was just around the corner. Lucas realized he should make some time to pack or else he'd be throwing things into boxes on the day of the move. He and Kate were supposed to be switching living spaces the day before the wedding and he had nothing ready to go. Maybe he could convince Bree to help him this afternoon after he got off work.

He was enjoying having Bree here. He didn't want it to end, but he also knew it couldn't continue. The wedding was coming right up.

He'd figure out a plan. The first step was to find Bryce and put an end to him terrorizing Bree.

Lucas knew the feelings he had for Bree were growing. It made him wonder if there might be another Grant family wedding sooner rather than later.

He whistled as he cracked another egg into the bowl and stirred.

THIRTY-SIX

Peter paced around his office. The wedding was days away. Practice with Fiona was getting better. He wasn't falling or stumbling now. At least not as much. While he was no Fred Astaire, he was more confident he could pull off the dance without completely embarrassing himself.

Thankfully, they were going to the reception hall after the rehearsal on Friday night for dinner. They would be making sure everything was set for the next day. Fiona saw it as a chance to practice one last time on the actual dance floor.

Peter ran his fingers through his hair making it stand on end. He wasn't as concerned about the dance anymore. No, now he was concerned about his heart. He enjoyed spending time with Fiona. More than he wanted to let on.

He'd never met another woman like her before. She pulled no punches and said everything she thought. He never wondered what she was thinking.

He shook his head. It was crazy. They got along well, that was evident during their evenings together, but he was the pastor of a local church. She was a vibrant, funny, gorgeous woman. They were as different as night and day. He was introverted, sometimes painfully so, while she was the extroverted life of the party. There was no way they were compatible.

He had counseled quite a few couples at this point in his ministry. One of the things all the literature emphasized was to find areas where the couple enjoyed the same things. It was important to find things to do together, commonalities. He couldn't think of a single thing he had in common with Fiona Gilliam. Nothing.

He also had no idea where she stood with spiritual matters. Yes, she came to church each week, but he knew better than most that didn't mean she was a Christ follower.

She certainly was becoming a distraction to him each Sunday though. He made sure not to look in her direction or he found himself losing his place in his sermon each time. It was becoming embarrassing.

He continued pacing his office. There was a light tap on his door, and he turned to see the woman he was just agonizing over walk into his office. He gaped at her. *Very funny, Lord. Very funny,* he thought to himself as he cleared his throat.

"Hey, what's up? I didn't expect to see you until Friday afternoon." Peter prayed none of the thoughts he had just been thinking showed on his face.

He watched as Fiona nervously brushed the front of her dress down as if brushing away some invisible lint.

"Fiona, are you okay?"

She jumped. "Oh, yes, of course."

Peter looked at her quizzically. "Can I help you with something?"

"I just wanted to stop in and see how you were doing. All ready for the big day?"

"I think so." Peter glanced up to see her staring at him.

"I'm glad we're going to run through the dance Friday. That should shake out the last of the nerves." Fiona glanced away.

Peter watched as a blush started to form on her cheeks. He loved it when she blushed. He realized he would love to spend a lot of time getting her to do it more.

"I certainly hope so." Peter fought the urge to clear his throat again. Instead, he ran his fingers through his hair, standing it on end even more.

Fiona looked up at Peter and replied, "You've got it down though. Just move with confidence and you'll be fine. You only mess up when you get in your head and start thinking about all the things you've done wrong in the past. Just stay in the moment."

Their eyes locked at those words. Without realizing it, Peter found himself suddenly standing right in front of Fiona. He had no memory of moving across the room towards her. "Right, stay in the moment."

The words came out hoarsely. His hand moved towards her hair, but he stopped before touching her. He wanted to rub a strand between his fingers but held himself back. Instead, he let his hand drop and keeping his eyes on hers said, "I can do that."

His eyes moved to her lips and back to her eyes. Slowly he leaned forward, closing his eyes, aching to finally know what her lips would taste like.

"Young man! What do you think you're doing? And you a pastor! My word. I should report you to the elder board."

The couple jumped apart as the loud voice broke the spell that had woven its way around them. Mrs. Johnson was standing in his doorway glaring at the two of them.

Of course, Mrs. Johnson had to come in through the office entrance rather than the sanctuary, Peter thought with regret. Maybe he needed to put an alarm on that door, too.

Peter cleared his throat and prayed it would hold up as he answered, "Mrs. Johnson, what can I do for you?" He was glad he wasn't blushing, but a quick glance showed that Fiona was blushing enough for both of them.

"I'll see you later, Peter." Fiona tossed the words over her shoulder as she hurried out the door. Their eyes met and Peter knew he was in trouble.

He was falling for this woman whether it was a good idea or not. And right now, he didn't really care. He wanted to throw caution to the wind for once in his life and see what would happen.

THIRTY-SEVEN

Tucking the last of her things into a box, Bree looked around to make sure she had everything she'd brought with her to Lucas and Drew's. She would be moving back to her apartment today. She wasn't sure she was ready, but it was time. Lucas would soon be moving into his own apartment. There was no way Bree was going to continue to live here after Drew and Kate were married. That would be beyond awkward.

It was a couple weeks since the note had arrived on her doorstep. She hadn't told Lucas that a second note was left on the counter at work just yesterday. She had no idea how Bryce managed that one.

When she went to clean up after a customer, there was a white notecard sitting under the plate. It simply said *I am watching*.

It took every ounce of self-control to not run screaming from the restaurant, jump in her car, and high tail it out of Haven right then. Where Bree would go, she had no idea, but she knew she couldn't continue living this way. The fear and uncertainty were causing her to lose sleep, lose weight, and it felt like she would lose her mind at times.

The part that scared her the most was she still hadn't seen him. No one had. She'd asked the patrons sitting around that section if they'd noticed who left the card. They couldn't recall anyone but the woman who had eaten there. That probably meant Bryce convinced the mystery woman to deliver the note.

Bree still had no idea how Bryce had found her. She'd been so careful when she left Connecticut to go north. She was even using cash exclusively. She wondered if he'd hired a private investigator.

She grabbed her phone off the charging cord on her way by to grab a few more things. It hadn't been holding power as well lately. She should probably take it in to get checked out, but she didn't have time. Time was running out. She felt like she was constantly in a state of fear, just waiting for Bryce to find her.

She couldn't deal with her phone right now. That was the least of her worries. She'd finally decided the only safe thing to do was leave. She needed to get on the road and soon. Her only hope was to stay ahead of Bryce and right now, she had no idea where he even was.

She hesitated. Was she doing the right thing? She was so tired of being afraid. What was it Peter said during his sermon on Sunday? *The Lord is for me; I will not fear; what can man do to me?*

She was tired of feeling afraid. Should she stay and fight? Would the Lord help her as He promised? She just wasn't sure.

She called out to Drew, who was working in the kitchen. "I'm heading out to work!" Lucas had made it abundantly clear she was not to go anywhere without telling someone when she left, when she arrived and, most importantly, where she was headed.

"See ya!" Drew called out in acknowledgment of having heard her.

Bree grabbed her keys and the last box. She opened the trunk and placed it inside with the others. Slamming it closed, she got in and turned the key.

She rested her hands on the steering wheel for a moment as she closed her eyes. She had been trying desperately to connect with the Lord.

The notes had shaken her so badly she had stopped everything, praying, reading her Bible. All of it. She was in survival mode and knew it. She also knew that doing life on her own wasn't working. Maybe it was time, past time, for some divine assistance. She needed to stop taking back control.

"Lord, help me to know what I should do. If I should run, guide me. If I should stay, help me. Make Bryce mess up. Help what he's doing in the shadows be brought into the light. Above all, keep those I love safe. Amen."

She opened her eyes and realized when she said "those I love" she instantly thought of Lucas. She knew her feelings were growing, but to be in love? She hadn't thought she would ever be to this point again. Yet here she was. In love. Fully.

Tears welled in her eyes. She wanted to stay and see where their relationship would go. What would a healthy relationship even look like? She didn't even know. She was so naïve when she had started dating Bryce.

She'd never had a serious boyfriend before. She spent so much time with her grandparents growing up that she had always been slightly awkward around people her own age.

Bree wasn't good at flirting. Social situations were difficult and casual conversations were often horrid. She'd always been shy and insecure. Even with Bryce she was that way. He'd seen it as another flaw, one of many he liked to point out from time to time.

Looking back Bree finally saw how dysfunctional her relationship with Bryce had truly been. It was even more apparent now in the light of her relationship with Lucas.

She stopped the line of her thoughts. There was something wrong with Bryce, something deeply wrong. She would not compare her relationship with Lucas to what she'd had with Bryce. It wasn't fair to Lucas.

There was something broken inside Bryce. Something that made him possessive and abusive.

She'd watch as he gave a subtle dig to a co-worker at the office. He'd never word anything so it was obvious, but if you listened and heard the inflection in his voice, you could tell when he was being sarcastic or disrespectful. He would always laugh it off so those around him would too.

Bree blinked back the tears as the memories crashed forward. She'd thought she'd been going crazy. There were so many little things Bryce had done to make it look like she was incompetent. She knew now how he'd been playing a sick game with her.

He'd enjoyed watching her squirm. She was like a mouse being played with by a cat. And he hadn't stopped. He was continuing with the game. Why couldn't he just let her go?

Bree glanced out the window and saw the little stone church just ahead of her. She put on her turn signal and decided to take a few minutes to spend time talking with God. She was thankful she had left a few minutes early for work. She wanted to be sure she wasn't being guided by her own emotions, but by what God wanted her to do.

THIRTY-EIGHT

Pulling up his sermon for Sunday, Peter regretted not finding someone else to preach this weekend. He wasn't sure what he had been thinking considering his family would start arriving soon for his brother's wedding. He couldn't remember the last time he'd taken a weekend off.

He'd only found help when he'd had a cold a couple of years ago and lost his voice. He could hear his parents now. "Peter, you need to take care of yourself. How else can you look after others?"

While he knew this to be true, he was too much of a perfectionist to let it go. He knew he needed to work on that character flaw, but right now, he needed to finish this sermon. Friday afternoon was no time to find a substitute to fill the pulpit unless it was an emergency.

He heard the door chime for the front doors go off and sighed. He looked up. "Lord, this has to stop. I know you're probably trying to teach me something here, maybe about my constant procrastination, but you are going to have to write this one again unless you keep everyone away for a few hours. I barely have an outline started let alone anything of substance to share. I could use some divine help and inspiration, please and thank you."

He pushed back his chair and rose to see if the person in the sanctuary needed him or not. For the thousandth time, he thought maybe the door chime hadn't been a good idea after all.

He walked out and saw Bree sitting in a pew with her head bowed. He approached quietly in his soft-soled shoes.

"May I pray with you?"

Bree's head snapped up and she gave a squeak of alarm.

"I'm sorry! I really need to stop doing that." Peter gave her an apologetic smile.

"It's okay. I just didn't hear you. I thought I was here alone. Well, just me and God anyway. We were having a little chat."

"Anything you want to share?"

"Just trying to get some life things figured out."

Peter saw the doubt in her face. He knew things were getting more serious between her and Lucas. She'd started coming up more and more in conversations with his brother. But if she was in trouble, or if she might hurt his brother, he thought he ought to know. Maybe he could help.

"What type of life things? I'm a pretty good listener. And a pretty good secret keeper, too." Peter smiled as he watched the doubt clear from Bree's face. She had the type of face that said everything she was thinking.

While Peter did want to protect his brother, he also would keep things in confidence. He would just get creative if there was something he needed to share to protect Lucas.

"Okay, I'm trying to figure out how to know what God wants me to do. How do I fully trust Him?"

"That can be difficult." Peter sat down in front of Bree and studied the windows beside them. He was relieved she wasn't struggling with her relationship with Lucas. This he could help with, he was sure.

He reached out an arm and pointed towards one of the windows. "What do you see there?"

Bree turned to look. The window showed a body of water with high waves. Jesus was standing on the water with his arm outstretched. There was another man shown from behind. He was up to his waist in water stretching a hand towards Christ.

"I see Jesus standing on the water and another man reaching out to him."

"You mentioned trust earlier and how you're struggling to trust the Lord to lead you."

He raised a hand and pointed at the window. "That is what this story is all about. Trust."

Bree looked at him quizzically. "How so?"

"Jesus and his disciples had been busy for days. The crowds grew everywhere they went. Can you imagine how tiring it must have been to have people clamoring at you, wanting something from you all the time, asking for healing?

"The disciples and Jesus had just fed well over five thousand men plus women and children so more like ten to fifteen thousand people.

"After they were done, Jesus had the disciples get back in their boat to head across to the other shore. Jesus went off to take some time to talk with his Father.

"Meanwhile, his disciples were in a small boat, in the middle of the Sea of Galilee. Sudden winds would come off the mountains surrounding the sea and cause waves, large waves. Some of the men were fishermen who had spent decades on that very body of water working. They were still terrified by this storm.

"The disciples had already been out on the water a long time. The sea had been battering their boat. They couldn't make it to shore. They were all scared, including the fishermen. Suddenly they see this figure striding by on top of the water. Whoever it was, was walking on top of the water. Now they were even more frightened. They thought they were seeing a ghost. Then Jesus calls out, 'It is I.'"

"I'm not sure that would calm me down any," Bree said dryly.

Peter laughed. "I'm not sure it would me either, but one of the disciples recognized the voice as Jesus. It was Peter. Basically, Peter has a moment of bravery and asks Jesus to tell him to come, to walk on the water to Him."

"I suppose that is one way to make sure it wasn't a ghost, but that's a little risky. I mean look." Bree gestured to the window. "It doesn't seem like it ended well for the disciple."

"He started off strong. He was walking on the water with his eyes fixed on Jesus. But do you know what happened?"

"Well, from what it shows there, he started to sink."

"Exactly. Peter took his eyes off Jesus and focused on the waves around him instead. That is when he began to sink in the storm-tossed sea."

Peter watched as Bree turned her eyes back to the window. He prayed his words were helping her. "The disciple Peter had done well when he was focused on Jesus and following His command to come to Him. It was only when his focus shifted that he got into trouble.

Bree was intrigued by the story. "What happened next? Did he survive?"

"Yes, Jesus saved him and even told the sea to settle down and it did. He also reprimanded Peter for his lack of faith and trust. If Peter had simply trusted Jesus, not only for who He was but also for what He had told him to do, he would have been fine."

"So, you're telling me to trust Jesus?"

"I'm not telling you. I'm showing you that God invites you to trust Him fully and completely. No matter what you're concerned about, He will sustain you and protect you. You just have to let Him. He will never force your trust. It's a choice you make. You can either stay in control of your own life or place your life in the hands of the God of the Universe, the one who loves you and created you."

Peter smiled as he realized the Lord had done it again. "Feel free to stick around as long as you'd like. I need to go finish my Sunday sermon."

He stood and headed towards his office quietly whistling under his breath. The Lord had once again delivered a sermon topic to him in the nick of time.

When Peter surrendered his plans to God's interruptions. God provided exactly what Peter needed. Always.

*****

Bree contemplated Peter's words as she watched the hall door close behind him. She knew deep down he had spoken truth. Jesus wanted her to trust Him, fully and completely but she was having a hard time reconciling that with her feelings about her situation.

Part of her was still inclined to run while part of her was saying to stay. Glancing at her watch, she saw she now had only about five minutes to get to work.

She stood and hurried out of the building, praying for God's peace, the same peace that had come over the waters, to come over her storm-tossed soul.

THIRTY-NINE

ryce tucked his SUV into the back of the lot and killed the lights. He hadn't been happy about switching to the larger vehicle, but after that old biddy had spotted him one too many times, he had no choice.

He settled in with his binoculars and began to scope out the entrances and exits. The large barn was situated with one end facing towards the tree line. There looked like there was a small parking lot nearby. The large double doors opened towards the driveway and faced the main parking lot. The entire building was tucked back from the road, so he was taking a chance being here. There was no other way to see what was going on. The driveway was long and winding and there was no view from the road.

He tugged the baseball cap down and sank lower into his seat. There would be more people tomorrow and less chance for him to be caught. Although, by the time he was done tonight, he would have a foolproof plan all worked out.

He smiled as he once more raised the binoculars to his eyes. Thankfully, it was dusk out and the shadows were lengthening. The dark colored SUV blended in well. He was counting on everyone being too busy to notice him parked at the back. He would have to time his leaving correctly, so no one noticed him.

He couldn't believe how easy it had been to follow her. Sabrina had never noticed that he had downloaded and activated a tracking app on her phone. It was a simple application which ran in the background. If her phone was on, he could find her.

She was forever leaving her unlocked phone laying around. It had been easy to install and activate the app without her knowing.

He had been so confident in her not figuring out what he had done that he had waited a full month before heading north to find her. By that time, she had been settled in Haven. It had been simple to find her.

He had been enjoying playing with her. The thrill of watching her without her knowing had been the best adrenaline rush. He had one more trick to play and then it would be time.

Soon he would remind her how their relationship wasn't over until he said it was. Bryce pulled the binoculars up to continue watching the people milling around the barn. Tomorrow night he would be back to grab her. She would be where she belonged. With him. Forever.

FORTY

Peter wiped his sweaty hands on the front of his dress pants. He stood just outside the back of the barn as the rehearsal dinner was winding down. How had he let Drew and Kate talk him into this?

A few months ago, it had seemed impossible. Then with Fiona's help these last few weeks, he thought he could pull it off. Now, tonight, even with mostly just his family here for the rehearsal dinner, he thought he was going to be sick. He just knew he was going to trip or even drop Fiona or… or… He wiped a hand down his face.

"Hey there, you doing okay?"

Peter whirled around to find Fiona looking at him with a wry smile on her face. "What? Oh, yeah. I'm fine. Just fine. Yeah. Fine."

Fiona laughed. "You're the furthest thing from 'fine' I've ever seen in my life, Peter Grant. And you," she poked a finger into his chest, "are a horrible liar."

Peter grimaced. If he couldn't fool Fiona about his inner turmoil, how did he ever think he would fool his parents. He looked over her shoulder at the mass of people inside. Maybe they would be so busy catching up, they wouldn't notice when they started dancing. He groaned. They would watch. He knew they would and this was only the practice. How was he ever going to do this in front of more people at the actual wedding?

His parents were here, of course. Jill and Ken would not miss a child's wedding for anything in the world. And this wedding was extra special. This wedding would finally make Kate a Grant, something his family had prayed about for a long time, ever since she had been a foster child of theirs years ago.

He watched his sister, Claire, bend down on one knee to talk with her son. He had been tormenting his sister and Claire was letting him know she had reached her limit. His nieces and nephews were enjoying running around like little banshees in the large barn. Their shrieks echoed off the rafters. He was thankful when he saw siblings and in-laws starting to rein them in. His head had started to pound with the noise.

"Hey, it's going to be okay. It's time. Kate wants to run through the dance for tomorrow. Ready?"

Peter sighed. "I guess it's too late to back out, isn't it?"

"Peter Michael Grant." Fiona raised one eyebrow at him and stood, hands on hips, giving him a mock glare.

Peter's head snapped up at the use of his full name, but then dropped when he saw the look on her face. He was trying to decide if he regretted giving Fiona that information or if he liked hearing her say it. He thought it was the latter but if he started to examine the thought too closely, he really would drop her on her head during the dance.

"Peter, look at me."

He found himself falling into the green eyes sparking fire back at him. "Yeah?" He couldn't have put together a coherent thought if he'd tried.

Fiona reached out and took both his shoulders and gave him a little shake. "We practiced this. You know the steps. Just relax already! It's your family. They aren't going to care if you mess it up. Have fun. Can you do that?"

"Relax. Have fun. Maybe." He shrugged his shoulders and gave her a small grin. "I'm sorry, Fiona, I have no idea why I'm stressing like this." He shrugged, "I just am."

Fiona rubbed her hands up and down Peter's arms. He liked the feel of her hands on him. It was not helping him think straight. Not one bit.

She dropped her hands and took a step back. Peter missed her touch already. "What did you just preach on this past Sunday?"

"Boasting in the Lord and not in yourself." He felt a gut check at the words and hung his head. He had been doing just that. He had been so worried about how *he* would look, he was forgetting it didn't matter. Fiona was right, he needed to relax and have fun.

Fiona reached out and placed a finger under his chin, raising it up. She stared into his eyes once more. "Does it really matter what happens? Don't let the fear of 'what if' rob you of the joy of right now."

Peter stared into Fiona's eyes and smiled. "Did anyone ever tell you how smart you are, Fee?"

"You can start anytime you want."

As she laughed, Peter felt his heart pick up speed. He realized he had just used her nickname for the first time.

"Now, let's do this!" Fee linked her arm with his and led him over to the large double doors.

Peter silently thanked God for the woman on his arm. They didn't have anything in common, but he was starting to realize that might not be as important as he once thought.

FORTY-ONE

Bree sat bolt upright in bed, gasping. She looked around trying to figure out where she was. She wasn't at Lucas's place.

She flopped back against the pillows as she remembered she was back at her own place. Lucas had moved into his new apartment. Kate would be moving into the cottage after she returned from her honeymoon with Drew. They would be getting married tonight.

Lucas still hadn't been thrilled to let Bree stay at her apartment, even with the new security system he had installed. They had argued quite a bit about it before she finally told him he needed to go home and so did she. If she was going to start trusting God, now seemed like the perfect time to start.

Lucas hadn't agreed with her staying there but had realized there wasn't a better solution. He'd refrained from following her home, but he demanded a call from her once she was safely there.

He'd insisted on giving her a canister of his police issued pepper spray. He told her it made him feel better, but she didn't see the difference between what she had been carrying and what Lucas gave her. Trusting God didn't mean she couldn't be proactive. At least she didn't think so.

Bree had finally stopped wrestling with her decision. She was going to leave. Tonight. Her plan was in place. She felt it was what God wanted. Even still, her heart sank at the thought of leaving.

She shook her head slightly. She couldn't start second-guessing herself now. She had written Lucas a letter and would leave it for him on the table. She knew Mr. Hill would let Lucas in when he came looking. And Lucas would come looking.

She brushed a tear from her cheek. It was the thought of leaving Lucas which had her slightly undone right now.

She pushed the covers back and headed to the bathroom to get ready for the day. As she brushed her teeth, she stared at her reflection. Was she really trusting God? She thought so, but it was so hard to know for sure.

She rinsed her mouth. No, she knew it was futile. Bryce had made it very clear she was not to leave him. Ever. At first, she'd taken it as a compliment. No one had ever treated her as well as he did in the beginning. He showered her with flowers and compliments. She'd thought he was so romantic.

It wasn't until she'd gone out to a paint night with some friends from work when she realized what he was hiding under his public persona.

The girls laughed and joked about their creations. They painted a little owl sitting on the branch of a tree at night. The painting hadn't been technical. It was almost like doing

326

a paint by number without the numbers. The instructor walked them through each little step.

Bree enjoyed getting to know some of the woman from work a little better. When she arrived home, her thoughts were on where she would hang her new creation. But Bryce was sitting on the couch, waiting for her.

She hadn't even had time to consider how he had gotten into her locked apartment before he went on the attack.

"I came over to see my girlfriend and find out she's out on the town with friends drinking the night away. Did I spoil your plans being here? Do you need me to leave so the guy waiting outside the door can come in?" He sneered as he rose and stalked towards her.

"What guy? What are you talking about, Bryce? We didn't have plans tonight. I went out with Joan and the other girls from work to a paint night. I thought I told you. I'm sorry if I didn't. See, I made this. Isn't it cute?"

Bree held up her painting to show Bryce as he continued towards her. "I had so much

327

fun." She hadn't realized the extent of Bryce's anger with her. She foolishly continued trying to diffuse the tension building in the room.

"Fun? You had fun while I sat here waiting for you."

The smile slid off Bree's face. She was confused. She distinctly remembered telling Bryce what she was doing tonight. He hadn't seemed upset at the time, but he certainly did now. She'd never seen him act like this before.

Bryce ripped the painting out of her hands and broke it in two over his knee. He ripped the canvas off the wood frame and tossed it all to the floor.

"Never embarrass me like this again, Sabrina. You will not go out at night without me or without my permission. Ever. Do you understand me?"

Bree stood in shock, not fully comprehending what was going on. What had she done wrong? She couldn't think of anything, but she knew she must have messed up somehow. "Of course, Bryce. I didn't mean to hurt you. I won't do it again." At least Bree hoped she wouldn't, if she could figure out what she had done in the first place.

Bryce stormed out and left Bree to pick up the pieces of the painting she had been so proud of moments ago and toss them in the trash.

The next morning a large bouquet of flowers was left on her desk along with a note that simply said, "I'm sorry."

That had been the start. The night of the paint night almost eight months ago. That was when her life had become scary and confusing. That was when she realized she had no control anymore.

She started refusing all the invitations her friends extended to go out with them. She always had an excuse ready. She never told anyone the truth though, that Bryce wouldn't approve.

It took a few more months until she realized she had lost herself. She had become a woman she didn't recognize.

She now stared at herself in her apartment mirror with her toothbrush hanging out of the corner of her mouth. Was she there again? Was she back to the point where she was trying to do something Bryce would approve of or was she trying to avoid the coming conflict?

She had become so good at it at one point. Now, she was just tired. Tired of making excuses. Tired of not feeling good enough. Just tired.

I am enough for you.

Bree stopped. Where had that thought come from? She looked around thinking maybe she had left her phone playing a video or music. She swiped it open and saw there was nothing playing.

She noticed the low battery notification and sighed. She'd forgotten to plug it in again. She would need to remember to charge it when she got in her car. Otherwise, she would have a dead phone by lunch.

Trust God, Peter had told her. She had been trying, but it didn't seem to be working. The

only way to protect herself was to go. The plan
was ready. Tonight, she would leave.

FORTY-TWO

S tanding with his hands on his hips, Lucas looked around his new apartment. He hadn't lived on his own since coming to Haven. It had been easier just to bunk with Drew than to try to find an apartment when he'd first arrived.

He willed the coffee to brew faster. He needed caffeine more than ever this morning after having a sleepless night. Even though Bree insisted she would be okay on her own, he sat outside her apartment watching until the wee hours of the morning.

Lucas had called in every favor he had to make sure someone would be nearby all night. It had been quiet. Thankfully.

After pouring a cup, he padded softly over to stare out the window facing the ocean. His thoughts were all over the place. One minute he was working plans in his head to find Bryce before Bryce lashed out at Bree. The next Lucas was trying to stay focused on the fact that Drew was getting married today.

He took another sip and realized he needed to turn it all over to God. It was obvious he couldn't fix this issue. It was bigger than him. He needed more help. And trying to control what he couldn't control was just making him distracted and fearful.

"God, you know what's going on. Keep Bree safe. Help us find this lunatic before anyone gets hurt."

Lucas took another sip, grateful for the caffeine. It was starting to settle his troubled thoughts.

He sat at the table and opened his Bible where he had left off reading. His eyes found Romans 8:28. *"And we know that God causes all things to work together for good to those who love God, to those who are called according to His purpose."*

"God, I don't know how any of this can be turned to good, but You do. I trust you Lord to do what it says here. I know You can work it all for Your good and for Your purpose.

"Please keep Bree safe. Help us to find Bryce before she gets hurt. Amen."

He felt the burden he'd been carrying lift slightly. Lucas needed to let God handle it because he knew he was incapable of doing it without His help.

And today Kate would finally become a Grant. Hmmm, maybe God really would work everything for good. If things hadn't happened the way they did with Kate all those years ago, she and Drew would be brother and sister, adopted siblings, but still.

He remembered the day Kate had arrived in their family all those years ago. She was close in age to his sister Sally and the two little girls had hit it off from the start. They had become fast friends and it had broken Sally's heart in two when Kate had gone back to her father. In fact, it had broken all their hearts.

Lucas took another sip of coffee as he thanked God for bringing Kate back into their lives after all these years. Today was going to be a good day. He could just feel it.

Lucas knew he had finally healed from his past heartbreak with Jillian. He had never thought he could move beyond his pain. But after praying, forgiving her, and asking God to heal him, he had experienced a real shift in his spirit. It was a feeling of freedom, and he hadn't even realized he was held captive before.

Whenever the hurt surfaced or jealousy threatened to rise up in him, he had been practicing giving it over to God. Lucas finally felt like his life was on the right track and Bree was a huge part of it.

A smile crossed his face. Tonight, he planned to tell her just what she meant to him. He couldn't wait.

FORTY-THREE

Peter thought he was going to be sick. It was go time and he couldn't form a single coherent thought. He could barely remember his name let alone the timing or steps for the dance.

He was literally hiding. He was such a coward. He'd talked a good talk about trusting God just this past week, even preparing a sermon about it. And now here he was, cowering behind the barn, hoping no one would notice.

He laughed to himself. He knew he wouldn't be able to hide, but right now, he could delay. Just a little. Just long enough to get himself under control.

"There you are!"

Peter jumped as Fiona came around the corner. Fee. She looked gorgeous in a green dress that matched her eyes. Her red hair curled around her shoulders. He couldn't take his eyes off her as she walked towards where he was leaning against the side of the building. He was pretty sure he stopped breathing.

"C'mon. It's time." Fee reached out a hand.

Without thought, Peter took it. He felt his breath release. A feeling of calm came over him as he looked at this woman in front of him. This bubbly, vivacious, fun-loving, energetic, wonderful woman.

"Thanks, Fee."

She gave him a puzzled look. "For what?"

"For being you. For teaching me how to dance. For making sure I'm not going to bumble this entire thing. Just, thanks."

He watched as a blush climbed up her face. He loved making her blush. He wanted to stand there all night just watching her.

Peter felt Fee tug on his hand. He sighed. "Right. The dance. I suppose they'll miss us if we don't show up, right?"

Fee tugged on his hand. Peter meekly followed her into the barn and stood beside Drew and Kate, waiting for their cue.

The lead guitarist in the band nodded to them, and the couples made their way onto the floor. Peter took a deep breath, and kept his eyes firmly fixed on Fee. "What if I stumble again?" he whispered to her as they took their places.

"You can do this. I trust you."

Peter's heart raced at the words. It was a feeling he'd never experienced before. This trust of a beautiful woman. He felt a smile cross his face.

"I couldn't do this without you." Peter relaxed as the song started. He caught the beat he needed, and they were off, whirling around the floor, hitting each step, each beat perfectly.

Peter didn't care what anyone, but Fee thought at the moment. He kept his eyes on her and no one else. Every tip and trick she had taught him over the last few weeks worked. He didn't stumble once. He even found himself smiling and enjoying every moment.

As the last note sounded, they struck the final pose. Fee, with an arm flung back, turned her head to look at Peter. Once more he felt his heart stop.

He stared at her lips. They were right there. He just needed to lean down. It would take just a moment to finally know what her lips would feel like.

He felt Fee put her arms around his neck. As he pulled her closer, he finally heard the applause and whistles coming from all directions. The noise was so loud it finally penetrated his utter focus on the woman in his arms.

Peter abruptly stood, pulling Fee up. He felt his face heat as he turned to see Drew and Kate locked in an embrace, kissing.

He glanced at Fee and began clapping along with everyone else. He thought he was blushing harder than Fee at the moment. He was thankful all eyes were on the newlyweds.

FORTY-FOUR

Groaning, Bree glanced at her phone. She was almost out of battery. She had been careful to keep it charged today, but the battery just wasn't holding the charge. It was now down to less than ten percent.

She watched as Lucas twirled his youngest niece around the dance floor in his arms. Little Esther was a chubby one year old. She squealed with delight with each spin. She started to dream about what it might be like to see Lucas holding their child.

She shook her head. It wasn't going to happen. Not with her leaving tonight. She wasn't going to linger over thoughts of what if. She'd made her decision. She was sure it was the right one. It had to be.

*****

Lucas bounced his niece in his arms as he twirled in a circle. He enjoyed being an uncle. He glanced over to where he'd left Bree and thought about what it might be like someday to be a dad instead of just an uncle.

At that moment Esther started to rub her eyes and Lucas headed off the dance floor and quickly deposited her in his sister's arms. He didn't do fussy and irritable. He was a fair-weather uncle and only did laughing and smiling.

"Here you go, Sally. All ready for bedtime." He winked at his sister as she reached to take her daughter.

"Thanks, Lucas. I think. You at least wore her out a little so hopefully she'll sleep better tonight than she did last night."

"Anytime." He turned to head back towards Bree. He was determined to get another dance with her tonight. His family had been monopolizing his time and he wanted to spend more of it with his date. He stood and scanned the room.

341

"Who is she?"

He jumped. He had been so focused on locating Bree he'd forgotten he was still standing near Sally.

Sally, however, had been watching him closely. Esther was now snuggled as comfortably as she could get in her mother's arms, trying to get as close as Sally's growing belly would allow. Lucas was always amazed at how large a woman got when pregnant. However, he was also wise enough not to voice that to his six-month pregnant sister.

"Who's who?"

"Who's your date? Unless you're looking for another niece or nephew to kidnap. In which case, Brynn is over there giving her father a hard time. I think she's about three seconds away from tossing herself to the ground and kicking and screaming if you were so inclined to go help him out."

Lucas glanced to the side. Sure enough. Brynn had the red face which proceeded one of her famous tantrums. He opted to let her father deal with her to the best of his ability. He had a woman of his own to catch.

At that moment, he spotted Bree. It looked like she was headed outside. A wide smile split Lucas's face and he started in that direction.

"Nice talking to you, Lucas. Let's do it again sometime soon."

"Sure thing, sis." He tossed a smile over his shoulder and kept walking. He completely missed the shake of her head and the wry smile on her face. She knew what it looked like when one of her brother's was love-struck and Lucas had all the signs.

Lucas tried to hurry across the dance floor. However, the band started playing "YMCA" and the floor was more crowded than ever. He would have done better going out the double doors and walking around the outside of the building.

Cousins, siblings, and friends all tried to stop him and get him to join as they sang along and danced. He laughed but didn't stop. He was determined to find Bree before the song ended. He hoped the band had a nice slow one planned after this crowd pleaser.

Just as he cleared the dance floor, he saw his Aunt Gertie waving to him. He couldn't be rude, although he really wanted to pretend, he hadn't seen her. He walked over to where she was standing.

"When are you going to tie the knot, dear? I saw you with a lovely girl earlier. Who is she?"

Lucas had to give the woman credit. Only this aunt would corner him at his brother's wedding and ask such an intrusive question.

"Just a friend, Aunt Gertie. If you'll excuse me?" Lucas smiled as he continued making his way to the door he had seen Bree duck out.

He expected to see her nearby but there was no one there but the caterers. Lucas looked in all directions. Had she somehow slipped back inside without him seeing her?

He walked over to one of the catering employees. "Excuse me, have you seen a young woman come out? She was wearing a navy-blue dress, has dark hair, and is a few inches shorter than me."

"Sorry, dude. I haven't seen anyone but you come out that door in the last five minutes." The man shrugged and grabbed the container of dirty dishes he had set on the ground and placed it in the van before heading back into the building.

Lucas stood, going quiet. Something was wrong. He knew he had seen Bree go this way. She couldn't have gotten far. Where was she? There was no sign of her.

It was like she'd vanished.

FORTY-FIVE

Lucas walked back into the barn scanning the crowd as he went. Bree had to be here somewhere. They must have just missed each other. That's what he wanted to believe, but something felt off.

He was trying not to be concerned. Bree had been quiet all night, rarely smiling. He'd written it off as nerves at meeting his large family.

He kept scanning the crowd. He still didn't see her, but he spotted Peter. He headed towards his brother. Peter was the most level-headed of all of them. He would be able to tell Lucas if he was imagining things or not.

"What's up? You look like you're ready to kill someone. If you forgot, this is a wedding. Only happy thoughts are allowed." Peter smiled at Lucas as he approached but now his smile died when Lucas didn't return it. "What's wrong?"

"I can't find Bree."

"Is that all? I know you're crazy about her, but you can't be tied at the hip all the time. It's not healthy. She probably just went to the bathroom. She'll be back in a minute." Peter gave his brother another smile.

"Something's wrong, Peter. I can feel it. She's been acting weird all night and now she's gone. I've looked everywhere. She's not here."

"Let's get someone to check the bathroom before you activate cop mode. She could just be hiding out in there for a minute to avoid the crowd."

Peter looked up and caught Sally's eye and waved her over. He quickly explained what was going on and asked her to check out the ladies room.

"Sure. I'll be right back." Sally hurried off to where the restrooms were located and was back sooner than Lucas would have liked. If

347

Bree had been in there, it would have taken longer.

"She's not in there. I even checked all the stalls."

Lucas started to think logically about what he knew for sure. The ex-boyfriend she feared. The note she found in her apartment. What if he had chosen tonight to take her? It would be the perfect cover. A busy event. Lots of people coming and going.

"I'm going to go look again. Let me know if you find her." He headed towards the front of the building where the parking lot was located. He wanted to see if Bree's car was still in the lot. She'd insisted on meeting him here tonight.

Just as Lucas reached the front doors, he saw Mrs. Johnson heading straight for him. He moaned under his breath. He didn't have time for her right now. His gut told him that Bree was in trouble, and he didn't want to waste any more time trying to find her.

"Young man! Young man! Come here."

Lucas dropped his head. There was no way he was going to be able to sneak by as if he hadn't seen her now. He detoured towards the older woman already working on how to extricate himself from her as quickly as possible.

"Mrs. Johnson, I'm sorry I have something I need to go check on. Something urgent." He made to move past her.

"Wait just a minute. I have something to tell you. It's important!"

Lucas was compelled to stop not only by her voice but by the vice-like grip she had on his arm.

He reached down and gently tried to pry her fingers off. "I'm listening, Mrs. Johnson, but please be quick. I need to leave."

"Well, I never! Maybe if you had done your job the first time around, I wouldn't be speaking to you now. And it's a miracle I *am* speaking to you. Some hooligan just roared out of the parking lot and almost hit me!"

Lucas perked up. Maybe Mrs. Johnson was helping him after all. "Did you see what they were driving?"

"Some big SUV thing. All black with no headlights on. It's a miracle I even saw them coming and got out of the way. They swerved coming at me and I thought they were going to hit me for sure."

"What else do you remember?" Lucas didn't think it was a coincidence Mrs. Johnson had almost been hit just after Bree disappeared.

"It looked like that incompetent waitress from the Three Cats Café was in the passenger seat. Now she's with an equally incompetent driver. Seems to fit." She sniffed her disapproval of the situation.

"Thank you, Mrs. Johnson. I'll get right on that." Lucas sprinted past her and bolted for his car. Bryce had a head start, but Lucas knew the area better and he had cops at his back.

Where would Bryce take Bree? Would he just leave the area? He wasn't sure. He needed to figure it out and fast. He was now sure Bree hadn't left on her own, not if she had been in this SUV as Mrs. Johnson claimed.

He started his truck, his mind whirling with possibilities. He threw it into drive and headed out of the lot. He passed Mrs. Johnson, mouth agape, as he roared by. He gave a little wave and hoped she would tell everyone what happened.

Backup. He needed help. He waited impatiently for his phone's Bluetooth connection to hook up. Then he punched the speed dial for the police department. He called in his concern and asked for help. The dispatcher promised to send the message.

"Lord, watch over her. Keep her safe. Guide me." Lucas mumbled the words under his breath as his hands tightened on the wheel and his foot pressed the gas pedal just a little harder as he sped towards the highway entrance.

351

FORTY-SIX

Bryce grimaced. He was focused on getting out of the parking lot fast, before anyone noticed anything. Suddenly an old woman, the same one that had been popping up everywhere over the last few weeks, was standing directly in front of him. He kept going straight, not caring if he hit her at this point. She deserved it. She had made his plan all the harder.

He felt the vehicle swerve as Bree reached over and tugged the wheel. Bryce struggled to correct the SUV. Once he had it back under control he reached over and backhanded Bree across the face. "Don't do that again. I told you your mine. We're going home."

He smiled as Bree cowered in the corner trying to get as far from him as she could in the small space. It was time she learned he was done playing.

Bryce sped along the main road. His plan had worked. Now to just put some distance between whoever might be foolish enough to follow. He almost hoped the cop Bree had been hanging out with would try to find him. That could be fun.

His breath quickened at the thought and adrenaline flooded his system. He'd enjoyed the game so far. He looked once more at Bree. His smile broadened as he headed towards the highway. Yeah, this was definitely going to be fun.

*****

Bree silently prayed for help. She had thought she was doing what God wanted by leaving, but it was clear she hadn't. She'd tried to solve the problem in her own way. She now asked God to forgive her. She'd been foolish. So foolish.

Trust me. She jumped slightly. The same small voice from before. What did it mean though? Did it mean she would be rescued? She didn't know. She just closed her eyes and continued to pray. She knew she wouldn't be able to get out of this on her own. She would have to trust God for help, like she should have done in the first place.

"How did you find me?" Maybe if she could keep Bryce distracted, she could figure out a way to get help.

"Easy, I put a tracking app on your phone."

Of course, he did, Bree thought to herself. *That's probably why my battery has been dying so fast.*

Bree opened her mouth to say something else when a loud bang sounded. Bryce fought with the steering wheel to keep control as they swerved from one side of the road to the other.

Bree closed her eyes and held on. She didn't know what had happened, but she knew it would only be moments before they crashed. *God, help me!*

Bryce finally managed to gain control and he guided the SUV off the side of the road. "Stay there," he growled as he jumped out.

Her fingers itched to open the door, but they were on a stretch of road with no houses. She didn't think she could outrun him, especially not in her dress and sandals.

Be still. She heard the voice once more and closed her eyes. *Be still.* It came again and she began to pray.

She jumped as her door was yanked opened. "The tire blew. Get out." Bryce leaned in and opened the glove box to grab a flashlight. He grasped her arm and yanked. Bree barely managed to get her feet under her before she fell.

Bryce was soon dragging her along the road at a hurried pace. He had a vice-like grip on her arm. Bree knew she wouldn't be able to escape easily. Not yet anyway.

Bryce turned down a dirt driveway partially hidden by a stand of trees. Bree kicked off one of her sandals close to the main road without Bryce noticing in the dark. She hoped it would be enough to point someone in the right direction.

They were headed for a small cottage not far from Drew's house. She had walked there once with Lucas after supper one night. There was a path that followed the shoreline and connected the two properties.

The small cottage was surrounded by towering trees on all sides, which hid it from the road. There was a small porch off the front. She could hear the horn of the lighthouse but couldn't see the water through the trees. The cottage was dark, deserted by its summer residents for the year.

I'm trusting you, Lord, to fight this battle for me. Please send help soon. Please. Bree prayed as she watched Bryce break a small window, reach in, and unlatch the door.

"After you," he said as he swept his hand to gesture her inside.

Bree thought briefly of bolting for Drew's house, but she knew no one was there and it would likely be locked. She had nowhere to hide. She would wait for whatever help God was going to send her way and would continue to pray it arrived quickly.

FORTY-SEVEN

Lucas realized if he took the road past Drew's on the way to the interstate, he would encounter less traffic. It would allow him to go faster since he wasn't in his cruiser. He prayed it was the right decision and wouldn't give Bryce too much of a head start on him. He'd been praying nonstop for God to help him find Bree before it was too late.

As Lucas started up the road past Drew's, he spotted a vehicle on the side of the road. He slowed when he saw it was a dark SUV with New York plates.

"Thanks, Lord. I don't believe in luck. I know this is all You."

He pulled in behind the vehicle. He tried to see if there was any movement inside, but he couldn't tell. He grabbed the gun from his ankle holster and slipped out the door, staying low as he came up beside the vehicle.

He stood slowly peering in the back window but could see nothing. He slowly moved his way down towards the front. Still nothing.

He saw the SUV sitting crooked. He walked around and saw the blown tire. No wonder it had been abandoned in plain sight.

Lucas ran back to his truck and grabbed a flashlight. He hurried down the road, scanning for anything that might lead him to where Bryce was hiding. He knew he should wait for backup, but he couldn't waste a single moment when Bree was in danger. He would have to trust God to be his backup right now.

He reluctantly slowed his pace so he could scan more carefully in the dark. He was coming up on the driveway about five hundred feet before Drew's. His flashlight moved back and forth as he slowly jogged, praying he wouldn't miss anything. There!

He hurried over and bent down. On the ground was a single sandal. He leaned down to see it more clearly. He remembered Bree wearing them tonight. He stood to consider what to do next.

He needed to let the Chief know where he was and what was going on. Bryce would be even more dangerous now that he'd had to ditch his vehicle.

He pulled out his cell and quickly dialed dispatch and identified himself. He requested backup as well as the warden service. He didn't know if Bryce was in the cottage or if he was trying to make his way through the woods. Either way, Lucas knew he would need more help. His one goal was to get to Bree before...

He let his thoughts trail off. He was not going to go there yet. Time to focus and get the job done. He jogged slowly forward, staying close to the tree line.

His gut was telling him Bree was close by. Lucas continued with his slow jog up the driveway, a look of determination on his face.

FORTY-EIGHT

Bree prayed as she watched Bryce move around the inside of the cabin. He was checking all the doors and windows to make sure they were locked. He looked out behind the curtains, but the darkness hid anything or anyone who might be coming their way.

Where are you, Lucas? Bree knew he was coming for her.

"You thought you were so smart thinking you could run away from me. Well, I proved to you how stupid you are. I told you no one else could have you and I meant it. You're going to come back with me tonight. I just need to figure out a plan. Sit there," he pointed at the couch, "and be quiet or else."

Bree moved to the couch. Bryce tried to switch on a light, but it was clear the power had been shut off for the season. She shuddered in the chilly air and felt so alone.

She watched as Bryce used the flashlight to look around. She didn't know what he was looking for. The beam cut across a cross stitch hanging on the wall. She caught a glimpse of the verse, John 1:5.

Bree struggled to recall what the verse said as Bryce's light went over it a second time. *"And the Light shines in the darkness, and the darkness did not grasp it."* Bree relaxed slightly as she felt God's comfort flow through her.

Bryce paced from window to window in the shadows. Bree slipped off her lone sandal and pushed it under the couch out of view. She perched on the edge. If the opportunity came, she was going to take a chance and run. She could hide in the woods until morning. She wouldn't go meekly with Bryce. She braced herself and waited.

"The plan would have worked. We should have been on the highway now heading south.

No one would have found us. It would have worked."

Bryce whirled around, knocking small items off the windowsill in front of him. Bree heard the tinkling of shattered items and looked down.

A small sand dollar had skidded across the floor and broken at her feet. The smaller shells inside, the angels it contained, lay next to her bare feet. She leaned down and picked them up, holding them in her hand, remembering what her grandfather had told her so long ago. "There's always something good to be found in our brokenness, something beautiful. We need to trust the good Lord to help us find it."

Bree smiled at the reminder. *Be still.* The voice came again. She clutched the shells in her hand. *Okay, Lord, I'll wait, but please hurry.*

Bree listened with half an ear as Bryce continued to pace and mutter to himself under his breath. She suddenly caught movement outside the window next to her.

She glanced over to see Lucas standing there with a finger over his lips. He motioned to her to get down and then he disappeared without a sound.

Bree closed her eyes and thanked God. Lucas had found her. She sat on the edge of the couch, ready to move.

Before she could take a breath, the front door crashed open, and Lucas came barreling inside heading straight for Bryce. Bryce hadn't been prepared for the sudden attack.

Lucas charged forward with his gun drawn. "Get down! Get down on your knees now!"

Bree sat frozen. This was a side of Lucas she had never seen before.

Bryce raised his fists, eyes wide and wild. Lucas snapped out a foot into Bryce's knee, lightning fast. Bryce collapsed with a cry to the floor. He tried to punch out, but Lucas stepped nimbly to the side and kicked Bryce square in the nose.

Bree watched as Bryce flopped onto his back, hands clutching his face. Blood seeping from between his fingers.

Lucas tucked his gun behind his back, and pounced on Bryce, flipping him quickly onto his stomach. He placed a knee and his back and pulled an arm up high.

"You okay?" Lucas was panting slightly from the effort.

Bree couldn't move. Hands over her face, she was still in shock at how quickly Lucas had taken control.

Bryce started to thrash. "That's enough!" Lucas pulled his arm up a little higher until Bryce stopped. "Stay still. It's over. You're not going anywhere."

At that point Bree heard sirens in the distance. Relief flooded her body at the knowledge it was finally all over.

FORTY-NINE

Lucas held Bree's hand as they walked along the beach. The sun was setting, and all felt right in his world. He looked over and smiled, glad to have this woman in his life. Although, he frowned at the bruise that still showed on her cheek from where Bryce had hit her.

He stopped walking and turned to her. "I'm sorry I wasn't there in time to stop you from getting hurt."

Bree looked up in wonder at this man standing in front of her. God had brought him into her life at just the right moment. She wasn't sure what would have happened if he hadn't arrived when he did.

"You were there at the perfect moment, Lucas. God was teaching me to lean on Him, to trust Him. I kept trying to do things my own way, like running away. I need to stop letting fear rule me and to learn to trust God fully in all things."

"In all things, huh? You're an amazing woman, Bree."

Lucas reached out to brush her bruised cheek gently. Pulling her forward, he placed a brief kiss on the bruise. He smiled at her, amazed again how he had found peace. Finally.

His nightmares about failing Antonio had begun to fade. He'd learned to trust and love again. God had done all Lucas had prayed for and more. The two continued on their stroll along the beach.

Suddenly, Bree stopped and bent down to scoop something off the sand. "Look!"

In her hand, she held a sand dollar. Small and round. Perfectly shaped. "I've never found one on the beach before." She smiled as she remembered once again how her grandfather had shared about the angels inside. God had reminded her of it the night Bryce had taken her. Now, she'd found one, her own reminder of God's love for her.

"Did you know they're a symbol of peace?" Lucas cupped his larger hand under hers as the two examined the sand dollar. It barely filled her open palm.

"Really? Peace. Hmmm, maybe God is giving me one more nudge." Her hand closed gently over her find and the two continued on their walk, hands swaying gently between them.

Lucas knew it was meant for him as well. Peace. Finally. He knew it wouldn't always feel this way, but for now he was content and that was enough.

*****

Bree smiled to herself. She was slowly learning to do better at trusting not only herself, but Lucas and, most importantly, God. She glanced over at Lucas, amazed once more by the man walking beside her.

God was showing her how a man should treat a woman. It wasn't anything like she had ever known. She felt cherished and loved. She was regaining her confidence. God had shown how faithful He could be.

She smiled, content with her life, enjoying the feeling of Lucas's hand intertwined with her own, and trusting God with the years to come.

WHAT'S NEXT?

We've seen two of the Grant brothers find love. Now it's Peter's turn. Will Fee and Peter get together in the next book or will they allow something or someone to get in their way. Be watching for book three in the Haven series, coming soon.

Follow me on Facebook:

https://www.facebook.com/evelyngracebooks

Check out my website for more information:

https://www.evelyngracebooks.com/

ACKNOWLEDGEMENTS

I can do all things through Him who strengthens me.
~Philippians 4:13

Writing a book is not a lonely endeavor. I want to thank the following people who have helped and encouraged me on this journey.

First, my family. They have put up with many missed meals, many missed activities, and much angst as I worked on scene after scene. Their encouragement and love helped make this story possible.

Second, my husband. He encourages and inspires me daily. And he's the best beta reader I could ask for. He helps me make sure I write the men in my stories "manly enough." If there are any mistakes, they are solely mine. Thanks, babe!

Third, to my fabulous writing friend, Robin. We've known each other a long time (longer than we've been able to call ourselves authors!) and it is only through your encouragement and cheerleading that I can finally call myself a writer. Thank you for all of your help and ideas.

Next, is my friend and editor, Molly. Doing life with you is awesome. Your support is critical to the final project. Thank you! And it's always a good excuse for lunch.

Thank you also to sweet Emma. Your enthusiasm and fabulous comments helped make this a better story.

I also have to thank my friend, Jane. She is getting more forgetful every day, but each time I see her, she always asks how my book is coming. I always want to give a good progress report, so thank you for asking me, Jane! It helps!

And last, but certainly not least in any way is my Lord and Savior, Jesus Christ. I am a new creation because of my relationship with Him. Thank You for helping me with each story.